Lethal
RECONCILIATION

DOBI CROSS

Luxhaven
Publishing

ISBN paperback, 978-1-958987-11-7

Interior & Cover Design by Luxhaven Publishing

Editing by JD Book Services

Proofreading by Lisa Lee Proofreading

To JC, Grandma D, and DC, whom I love more than life itself.

AUTHOR'S NOTE

Thank you for choosing LETHAL RECONCILIA-
TION. Zora Smyth was a character that I was fortu-
nate to meet about a year ago as I brainstormed ideas
for my first medical thriller story for an anthology.

LETHAL RECONCILIATION continues the story of
Zora Smyth as she searches for her sister and deals
with the aftereffect of what she'd been through. We
see how Zora remains true to doing the best for her
patients while keeping her friends and family close
and safe.

It was important for me as I penned this series to
have Zora Smyth not be some super hero or a person
with extraordinary abilities, but an everyday person

who through the journey of the next few books comes to fully understand and appreciate who she truly is and is able to heal from the childhood baggage she's carried all her life.

Please continue this journey with me in LETHAL ADHESION. You can grab your copy at https://dobi-cross.com.

Would you also want to be notified when the next Dobi Cross book releases? Sign up at https://dobi-cross.com.

Once again, thank you so much for purchasing LETHAL RECONCILIATION and for meeting Zora Smyth. If you enjoyed it, please consider leaving a review at your favorite retailer or recommending it to a friend.

Thanks again for your support!

Dobi Cross

Lethal
RECONCILIATION

1

The young man in scrubs slipped into the Intensive Care Unit cubicle filled with the faint smell of life amid the aura of death and glared down at the man lying unconscious on the hospital bed. A tube snaked from the patient's mouth, and an IV line extended from his left forearm. His chest rose and fell in sync with the rhythmic beep of the cardiac monitor, though his breaths were slow.

"You old bastard," the young man whispered to the patient. "So you want to live after what you've done? Well, that won't happen."

He extracted a syringe and needle from his medical coat, pricked the IV bag with the needle, and emptied the contents of the syringe into the bag before increasing the IV line's flow rate.

Then he slipped out of the ICU the way he had come, hoping to be far gone before they discovered the patient was dead. The young man hastened down the hallway and into the stairwell, stripping off his disguise as he raced down the stairs. By the time he arrived on the ground floor, he looked like any other visitor to the hospital instead of the doctor he'd pretended to be. Even the glasses were gone.

The young man exited the hospital's main entrance and hurried to the next street over, where he discarded the disguise items in a dumpster that was about to be emptied by the garbage crew coming down the street.

Then he walked away.

Sixteen down, four more to go.

———

Andy Pratt felt adrenaline rush through his veins as his gloved finger hovered over the computer key. It was a powerful feeling, knowing he could exact vengeance on these bastards with just a single stroke.

He exhaled and hit the computer key, the sound snapping in the air with a note of finality. Andy watched as a brief message flashed across the computer screen and then disappeared.

It was done. In a few days, the man would be dead—it was what he deserved for the atrocity he'd committed.

Andy looked around the small apartment. The place was a dump, the nausea-inducing stench a testament to that, but it was perfect for his work—no one cared whether he came or left, though he remained cautious by changing his disguise often. He could never be too careful.

He packed up the laptop and its accessories into the only suitcase in the space before dumping all other items into a large trash bag. Andy would ditch the trash in one of the public waste disposal drop-off locations in a neighboring town. The suitcase would go with him to his next place, which was already prepared.

Andy glanced once more around the apartment to make sure he'd missed nothing. It was empty, ready for the next tenant.

He picked up his belongings and stepped out of the place.

Number seventeen, primed for death.

Alisa Petrykin dropped the flowers on the headstone and straightened. The morning air felt chilly, forcing her to wrap her fall coat tighter around her frame.

She was here to say goodbye to her brother, Thomas Stewart. Thomas—maybe she should call him Stewart like everyone else did—had kept his mother's maiden name and never taken the family's last name. Surprisingly, her father had never pushed for it, even though Stewart was his biological son. But all that hadn't mattered, more so now that he was lying six feet under the ground.

Everything about Stewart's death had been so hush-hush. Alisa didn't know how he'd died, and her father's men must have been on some gag order, because all conversations about Stewart ceased anytime she passed by. Her father had even forbidden her from attending his funeral, insisting he was protecting her from their enemies. Alisa had obeyed him and stayed home, though she disagreed with the decision. Thankfully, he'd given his permission for her to visit her brother's grave this morning.

Alisa felt a tightness in her chest. She still found it hard to believe her brother was gone—well, her foster brother, as Stewart had liked to remind her. It was only a week ago that he'd given her his usual icy stare when they ran into each other at home. Only her one-eyed chihuahua, Sparky, had brought the hint of a smile to his lips. Stewart wasn't a poster boy for good behavior; he'd scared her sometimes and had made it clear he hated Alisa, yet he was still her brother.

Now he was dead.

Tears rushed to Alisa's eyes, and she blinked them back. She missed him. Stewart had been her only sibling, and that mattered more than anything else. Even Sparky seemed to know he was gone— he'd refused his food from the day Stewart had died, and only a visit to the vet and lots of cuddles had gotten him eating again.

Stewart had also been a shield for her. As heir-apparent of their Russian crime family, he'd been the natural target, but now that he was gone, Alisa could sense the vultures gathering around her as the only other child of Anatoly Petrykin.

Some family members wondered if Anatoly was going to select her as the new heir, since she was heavily involved in the legitimate side of their business, even though her father had allowed no woman to hold a prominent role in the family. A few others even thought she was up for grabs. Even Vaslav, her father's right-hand man, seemed emboldened by Stewart's death to show interest in her, and she'd caught him staring at her a time or two.

But Alisa had no interest in taking over the family business and was not a prize to be plucked by some power-hungry subordinate who didn't know his place. She detested the crime world, though she cared for her family. That feeling motivated her to work hard each day to turn the family's legitimate businesses into profitable ventures. Hopefully, one day, those businesses would be enough for the family to sustain itself, without resorting to violence. Besides, her father was still a traditional man and would never allow a woman to lead the family, despite how much he loved her. He probably had a plan in place to select his successor.

But what occupied Alisa's mind was finding out who had killed her brother. How could she claim he was family when she didn't know how he'd died? *I'm a lawyer, for goodness' sake!* Shouldn't she, at a minimum, confirm if justice had been served for her brother?

She looked up to see the clouds had parted, and the sun had burst through in its glory, the very antithesis of how she felt.

Alisa let out a sigh—she'd stayed too long already, and it was time to leave. She adjusted her bag's shoulder strap and headed back to the parking lot. Her father's bodyguard must have seen her because the car started rolling in her direction.

Then Alisa noticed a striking young woman in a stylish luxurious black dress and a gorgeous fascinator leaving another headstone and walking away. *So someone else had also come to pay their respects to a loved one,* she thought. She watched as a middle-aged man joined the young woman and then escorted her into a black limousine that soon rolled through the parking lot's exit and toward the cemetery gates.

Alisa's car reached her at that moment, and she got in.

It was time for her to leave as well. Alisa was pretty sure her father was waiting.

Zora Smyth raced to where her mom stood.

"Mom, what's wrong?" Zora asked. Her mom, Adrianna Smyth, owner of one of the biggest law firms in the city, was a master at keeping calm in most situations. It was rare to see her so out of it.

Zora's mom stayed mute and continued shaking like a leaf.

Zora shook her mom's arm. "Mom, you're scaring me. What's going on?"

Her mom grabbed onto Zora for strength.

"What is it? Tell me," Zora insisted.

"I think…" her mom said.

"Go on."

"I think I just saw your sister."

Zora's heart rate sped up, and her eyes searched the cemetery grounds. Her sister had been missing for many years, way before Zora went to college, completed medical school, and started her surgical residency, though they hoped she'd show up one day. "Where?" she asked.

Her mom pointed a shaky finger toward the parking lot.

Zora dropped her handbag and took off running in that direction. Could it really have been her sister, or was her mom mistaken? No, it couldn't be false—her mom paid great attention to detail.

As she approached the parking lot, Zora noticed a black limousine leaving through its exit with what looked like a lady in a hat in the back seat. But the car was too far away for Zora to see the features obscured by the hat.

"Stop!" Zora shouted at the car as she rushed after it.

But the car sped up instead and raced toward the cemetery's exit.

She squinted at the license plate, but the numbers looked blurry, and soon the car exited the cemetery and disappeared from view.

Zora came to a stop, her chest heaving as she tried to catch her breath. She was too late, and now she'd lost the first real clue since her sister disappeared many years ago. No, make that the second real clue—the letter in her handbag which she'd just received, written by Kelly, an ex-convict who'd saved Zora's life in the detention center, was the first.

She hurried back to where she'd left her mom, who had slumped on the ground with her head buried in her hands.

"Mom, are you okay?" Zora asked as she reached her side.

Her mom looked up and grabbed Zora's arm. "Did you find her?"

Zora's shoulders slumped. She'd disappointed her mom. "I'm sorry."

Her mom's hands fell away. "It's not your fault," she said in a weary tone. "I shouldn't have frozen. But, Zora, I'm pretty sure it was your sister. She looked just like I did at your age."

Zora didn't know what to believe. Could it be that her mom was so distraught by the death of Marcus, who had been like a son to her, that it had triggered the memory of her lost sister? Zora shook the thought away. No, it had to be her sister her mom had seen— it was better to cling to that hope than let it go. Besides, her mom would never have such a reaction to just anyone.

"We'll find her, Mom," Zora said. She'd noticed the CCTV camera at the cemetery gates. Maybe they could get the license plate number from it.

Zora pulled out her phone and speed-dialed Marcus' number. Then she remembered Marcus, her friend and big brother, was gone, and her heart squeezed in pain. She wasn't sure if she would ever get over his death.

"What is it?" her mom asked.

"Nothing," Zora said, forcing a smile onto her face. She took a deep breath and then dialed Silas Park's number. Silas was her mom's right-hand man at her firm, and a high-profile criminal attorney with extensive connections. He would know what to do. Silas picked up on the first ring.

"Hello, Zora," Silas said from the other end of the line.

Zora stepped away from her mom. "Silas, we need your help." She explained what had happened and also told him about the letter.

"I'll get on it right away," he said. "How is your mom doing?"

Zora glanced at her mom, who had now gotten up from the ground and was dusting off the dirt from the back of her skirt. "Not too great at the moment, but I'm sure she'll be fine soon."

"Could you take her home instead? I'm not sure it's a good idea for her to show up at the office feeling the way she is. I'll head there now and wait for you."

"Sure, I'll do that. Thanks, Silas." Zora had sensed there was now more to the relationship between Silas and her mom. *About time if you ask me.* Silas had been by her mom's side since Zora's father had passed away many years ago. Her mom would be in excellent hands.

"My pleasure," Silas said. "See you soon."

Zora ended the call and turned to her mom. "Let's go," she said.

She would tell her mom about Kelly's letter later. For now, it was more important to get her home in one piece.

Hopefully, they would find a good lead from the CCTV footage.

And maybe, just maybe, they would finally find her lost sister.

"Why don't you come in?" Zora's mom asked as they parked in front of the large, stately home Zora had grown up in.

"Mom, I need to go," Zora replied.

"It would only be for a minute."

Her mom looked tired. It wouldn't hurt for Zora to stay for a while. "Okay, I will," Zora said. "Why don't you go ahead? I'll be right behind you."

Her mom nodded, stepped out of the car, and headed toward the front entrance.

Zora leaned against the car's headrest. Who would have thought today would bring long-desired clues about her lost sister? Maybe it was time for her sister to come home. Zora prayed with all her heart that it was true. There would be nothing like having her family complete again.

She would have loved to sit there and further dissect everything that had happened, but her mom was waiting, so Zora got out of the car and locked it. The air was quiet now that the security team hired after her release from the detention center was gone. Zora could see Silas' car parked out in front as well, which meant he was inside with her mom. Hopefully, he'd gotten some information already—her mom's firm resources were quick like that.

Zora reached the front entrance. She placed her hand against the sensor on the wall and heard a beep as the steel door her mom had installed after her sister's disappearance opened. She strode through the large foyer, the walls of which were covered with her father's watercolor paintings, and entered the living room.

Her mom and Silas sat on the large brown leather sofa that dominated the space. They dropped their held hands as soon as they spotted her.

Zora hid the smile that tugged at the corners of her lips. Her mom must feel weird displaying such affections in front of her grown-up daughter. But Zora didn't care—all that mattered was her mom was happy.

She took the loveseat opposite them.

"Hello, Zora," Silas said, breaking the uncomfortable silence.

"Hi, Silas. How's work?" Silas was in his usual immaculate three-piece suit. Zora had never seen him dressed otherwise in all the years she'd known him.

"Good," he said.

"Zora, do you want anything?" her mom asked.

Zora shook her head. "I'm good." She wasn't hungry. Besides, she was more interested in learning if Silas had found any leads. She turned to him. "Did you find anything?" Zora asked.

Silas shook his head. "Nothing we could use from the CCTV."

Zora stiffened. "Not even a license plate

number?"

"We got both from the footage, but the numbers don't exist. They're not registered to any car in the state, even though they look like ours."

Zora looked at Silas quizzically. "Both?"

"Two black limousines, instead of one, passed through the gates around that time, and neither license plate exists," Silas said.

"What?"

"I know. I didn't expect that either."

Interesting. "So, what's next?" she asked.

"No definite plans yet. We tried looking up other CCTVs in the area, but none captured the faces of the people in either car. It was like they knew what roads to take to avoid the camera. But we'll keep searching."

Zora's heart fell. Another dead end. But who were these people that were going to such lengths to hide their identities? Then she remembered Kelly's letter. "Did you find anything about the inmate in the letter?"

"What letter?" her mom asked, looking from Zora to Silas.

Zora pulled the envelope from her bag, pulled out the note, and handed it over to her mom. She watched the blood drain from her mom's face as she read it.

"Mom, are you alright?" Zora asked.

Her mom waved her concern away. "I'm fine. When did you get this?"

"That's the office mail you gave me at the cemetery."

"Oh. I should have…"

"It's alright, Mom. You didn't know." Zora turned back to Silas. "Any news?"

"We found out who she was," Silas responded. "But she was dead, like Kelly had written. The woman had no family, so now we're working to track down any ex-lover or close friend she might have confided in. I'm hoping we get something there."

Zora's shoulders relaxed. It wasn't all bad news— maybe they'd find something soon. She'd take this little progress in finding her sister any day over no news.

Her eyes strayed to the clock on the wall. Goodness, it was time to leave and prep for her return to work tomorrow. Zora was looking forward to taking care of patients again, while keeping out of any drama at the same time. It was what she needed and what Marcus had wanted for her.

Hopefully, her life at work would be peaceful here on out till she finished her residency.

"Here you go, Mr. Connelly," the fresh-faced nurse said as she handed him his discharge packet.

Sean Connelly let out a sigh of relief as he accepted the envelope. He could now leave the ER. Even though he'd been here for less than twenty-four hours, it had seemed like a week. Luckily, his wife had been around when the worst abdominal pain he'd ever felt had started and had rushed him to Lexinbridge Regional Hospital, where he'd received immediate medical care.

It turned out he had gastric ulcer, and the doctors had diagnosed him with a 'heli-something' infection, which the senior doctor assured him was treatable. His other symptoms had disappeared as well, so Sean didn't see the need to remind the senior doctor about them. He was just thankful he'd avoided being admitted.

Sean pulled out the sheets of paper from the large envelope and gave them a cursory look to satisfy the nurse. He'd never understood this medical jargon, and reading them gave him a headache. Thankfully, his wife, Susanna, was better at these things. But she'd stepped out to use the bathroom. Maybe she'd study them once they got home.

Home. He was looking forward to being back in his own space. Sean couldn't wait to eat the sumptuous dinner Susanna had prepared for him.

Hold on. Hadn't he received a call from one of his guys during his last dinner at home? What was it he'd said? Sean racked his brain. Yes, something about an attack, but he couldn't remember the details. All Sean's focus at the time had been on Susanna's pork crown roast with mushroom dressing staring him in the face, so who could blame him? He'd ended up in the ER shortly after and had only remembered the conversation now.

But who would have the audacity to attack Sean or his friends? They were the untouchables and could do as they pleased. It was more likely a false alarm— the guy who called was a known worrywart and hadn't bothered to ring back since, so the whole thing couldn't be as important as he'd stated.

"Do you have questions?" the nurse asked, bringing Sean back to the present.

"No. Everything looks good," he said.

"Great. Someone will be here to wheel you to your car."

"Oh, I don't need that," Sean said. "I'm sure I can walk to the car just fine."

"It's not a bother," the nurse insisted. "We're happy to do it."

Sean acquiesced. Either way, he'd be eating Susanna's fried chicken soon, inhaling its spicy fragrance instead of the antiseptic aroma he'd breathed in here. His mouth was already watering just thinking of the many more delicious meals she'd promised him over the next few days.

That was what really mattered, and nothing was going to stop any of it.

Anatoly Petrykin, head of the East European criminal enterprise in Lexinbridge, stared out at the shrubbery that hid most of his window from open view. This was the one day he wished he could see the clear horizon, even though he'd commissioned it to prevent the feds from having a bird's-eye view of his office.

He sighed. It was still surreal that Stewart was gone. He'd had no affection for his son, but Anatoly had been proud of him as a worthy successor who could lead the family with an iron fist. Stewart had only displeased him when he'd seen Stewart treat Alisa like a stranger instead of the sibling she was. He'd never addressed it, however, since Alisa would be out of the house by the time he handed over the family business to Stewart—Anatoly had already made the arrangements to ensure it.

But Stewart had been murdered. What was worse was Anatoly couldn't even pursue his revenge now.

He crushed the beer bottle in his hand and the bloodied pieces scattered on the floor. Even boiling Stewart's bodyguard, Erik, who had failed in his duty to protect his son, to death in a hot cauldron, hadn't been enough to assuage his anger. But Anatoly had to hold back his lust for revenge for the family's sake, even though he knew his rival, Uncle Jimmy, had killed Stewart. The feds' eyes were on him right now, and any wrong move from him could crash everything he'd built over the years. But Anatoly hadn't been called 'Snake' in his younger days for no reason —he could lie low for as long as needed and then strike when least expected.

For the time being, it was more important to make sure his family stayed in line. Though Vaslav tried to hide it, Anatoly had noticed his moves to secure additional power in the family for himself. But Anatoly wasn't worried. He'd made plans for this eventuality, though he hadn't imagined he'd need it. He'd almost burst an artery when he'd noticed Vaslav eyeing his daughter, and only the knowledge that it might fracture his family right now and put Alisa at risk prevented Anatoly from shooting him between the eyes. Anatoly was only keeping him around because Vaslav was still useful, but that would change once Anatoly decided it was time.

There was a knock on the door, and Anatoly turned in its direction. It had to be someone willing to risk his ire, since he'd passed down the order he was not to be disturbed unless absolutely necessary. There were only two people who fit the profile—Alisa and Yegor, his bodyguard. Anatoly pulled his handkerchief from his pocket and wrapped it around his bloodied hand.

The door swung open and Alisa stepped in.

His heart warmed at the sight of her, and Anatoly smiled. This precious daughter of his. When he'd first stared into her beautiful eyes, he never would have thought she would bring so much joy into his life. He'd never imagined he would have such tender feelings toward another human being, but it had happened with Alisa.

Anatoly frowned. He shouldn't be thinking such happy thoughts with Stewart still fresh in the grave. Anatoly owed him that.

He placed his injured hand behind his back and beckoned Alisa to come in. She looked paler than the last time he'd seen her—Stewart's death must have hit her harder than he'd expected. Maybe he needed to pay more attention to her, especially since she was all he had left now.

"Hello, Papa," Alisa said as she came to where he stood and tiptoed up to give him a kiss on the cheek.

"Solnyshko." *My little sun*. He motioned for her to grab a seat. Alisa tucked herself into the visitor's chair opposite him. Anatoly sat behind his desk and kept his wrapped hand out of view.

"Did everything go alright?" he asked.

"Yes, it did," Alisa said.

"You should eat more."

She gave him a small smile as she brushed a tendril of her honey-colored hair away from her face. "I'm fine," she said.

"What do you want to know, Solnyshko?"

Alisa's eyes widened. "How did you know?"

"I can read your face like a book."

Anatoly watched the myriad of emotions cross her face as she hesitated to speak what was on her mind. He could tell she was ready when she straightened her shoulders.

"How did Stewart die?" she asked.

The muscle in Anatoly's jaw twitched. She could ask everything else but this. "The topic is not up for discussion. Was that all?"

"Why? What would it hurt for me to know how he died? It's not like I'm going to seek revenge or anything."

Anatoly's anger spiked, and he jumped back to his feet. He knew his daughter well enough. She loved standing up for others; had been that way since she was a little girl. Sure, she wouldn't seek revenge, but she would pursue justice for Stewart as his only sibling. Anatoly didn't need the attention that would bring. "I want you to stay out of it! Do you understand?"

A blank expression dropped over her face as she stood. "Yes," she said simply.

Anatoly groaned—she was shutting him out. Alisa only did that when she didn't get something that was very important to her. That didn't mean she would give up either, no matter how obedient she sounded right now.

"I'll see you later, Papa," Alisa said, and left his office.

Anatoly sank back into his chair and ran his uninjured hand through his salt and pepper hair. He would have to keep an eye on her. Couldn't Alisa tell it was for her own sake? How could she not understand her father's heart? It would do more harm than good for her to go poking the hornet's nest.

He'd already lost Stewart; he couldn't afford another tragedy.

Losing Alisa would break his heart.

———

Anatoly was back at the window. Even reading the business documents on his desk hadn't been able to distract him. He wasn't sure what Alisa was going to do, but it couldn't be good.

He heard his door open, yet he didn't turn. Anatoly could tell it was his bodyguard, Yegor, from his somewhat silent steps. "How did it go?" he asked.

"There was some woman and that Dr. Zora Smyth at the cemetery while we were leaving. I think they might have seen the princess visiting the grave."

The muscle in Anatoly's jaw twitched. Dr. Zora Smyth again. He would have taken care of her for the role she played in Stewart's demise had the feds not been watching him. With her being so popular in the media lately, her death would draw a lot of scrutiny.

"Anything else?"

"There was another lady there with a bodyguard who left around the same time. I had them followed as a precaution. They entered a carwash a few streets away from the cemetery and came out later with a fresh set of license plates."

Anatoly glanced sharply at Yegor. "Have you seen them before?"

Yegor shook his head. "They didn't seem like they were from another crime family, and the name on the headstone the woman visited was not one I recognized." Yegor had a photographic memory and was well-connected in the criminal underworld. If he didn't recognize them, chances were they were of no interest or concern to Anatoly. But he would take precautions just in case.

"Get rid of the car and the license plates," he said. "And keep an eye on Alisa. I don't want her looking into Stewart's death."

"Yes, boss," Yegor responded and then left as silently as he had entered.

Anatoly let out a long exhale. This was not the time for any mistakes.

Alisa and the family had to stay safe, no matter what.

6

Alisa plopped on her bed in the cavernous suite that was her apartment and dropped her handbag beside her. She'd taken the rest of the day off, so she didn't need to head into the office. She took a series of deep breaths. But it did nothing to calm her down.

She was still mad at her father. Why was he being so unreasonable? It was her brother's death, for goodness' sake, and not something she could just gloss over! Alisa had seen the anger in his face at her question, but there had been something else she hadn't expected—a hint of fear.

She'd never seen her father afraid from the time he'd adopted her after her mother, the woman he'd loved, died, or so she'd been told since Alisa had no prior memories. What was he scared of? Fine, she was a target for her father's rivals, but that was nothing new. What else could it be? It wasn't like she was going to do anything that would endanger her life. She wasn't that stupid.

Alisa sighed. Her father must have found it strange that she'd insisted on digging into Stewart's death, considering how he'd treated her. But family was everything to Alisa, and Stewart had been part of it. Even Sparky seemed to have recognized that. *By the way, where is that naughty fellow?*

She searched the suite for him. Sparky was nowhere to be found. He was a homebody and loved to hang out with her, but Sparky had been acting strange of late. So if he was not here, there was only one other place he could be.

Alisa left her place and headed toward Stewart's room. As she expected, Sparky was outside the door, curled up in front of it. Alisa bent and lifted his sleepy figure into her arms.

Then she noticed the door was ajar. Stewart had been fastidious about locking his room, and it'd been that way this morning when she'd found Sparky there. So why was it open?

Alisa had never been in Stewart's room and wanted to see what it looked like. Maybe she would learn more about who Stewart had been, beyond what she already knew.

She pushed the door open, and it swung back. Alisa entered to see a much larger room than hers in muted blue with grey furnishings and the occasional burst of red. It was a strange color scheme for someone who was always dressed in black except for when he was heading into work at the hospital. She still didn't understand why he'd chosen to be a doctor —it wasn't the typical career path for future crime bosses.

She wandered further into the room till she entered what must have served as an office for him at home. The alcove was bare except for a desk and a chair and a few other items which were in disarray. There was a rectangle in the dust on the surface of the desk where a computer monitor might have stood. It was like someone had visited the place in a hurry. Alisa assumed the person had done so at her father's command, since she doubted anyone would be bold enough to enter Stewart's room without his permission. Had he removed it because he guessed she might come here? She'd only left his office a few minutes ago!

Alisa's mind whirled. There had to be something

about Stewart's death that her father was desperate to keep from her.

Then Alisa remembered a conversation she'd overheard many years ago between her father and Stewart about a secret tunnel in his room for emergencies. She was pretty sure her father had mentioned the alcove. Alisa wondered if it was real as her eyes searched the space, but nothing stood out.

Out of the corner of her eye, Alisa spotted something white sticking out beneath the back leg of the chair. What was that? She placed Sparky on the floor, stepped around the desk, and bent down to study it. It looked like the edge of a wallet-sized photo, so Alisa lifted the leg of the chair and picked the picture up.

The face of a pretty young lady in a grey turtleneck stared back at her. She was smiling at something beyond the frame of the photo, like someone had taken her picture without her knowledge.

Alisa's forehead wrinkled as she examined the photo. Who was she, and why was her picture in Stewart's room? The face looked familiar. Where had she seen it?

Then it came to her as she'd known it would. She'd seen the lady on TV last week!

Dr. Zora Smyth. Yes, that was her name. She'd been a suspect in the murder of a doctor who worked in the same hospital as she did. Wait! Wasn't that the same hospital where Stewart had worked?

Alisa studied the photo again. The lady didn't look like a killer, but looks could be deceiving. But why was her picture in Stewart's home office? Besides, the paper looked wrinkled, like Stewart had handled it multiple times.

Her eyes widened. Had she been his girlfriend? Alisa had never seen Stewart with any woman, but that implied nothing. If she was, had Stewart been involved in her case?

She made to put back the photo from where she'd taken it, but then Alisa changed her mind and slipped it into her pocket instead. Maybe this was the clue she needed as the first step in unraveling the truth behind Stewart's death, and she knew the perfect man to help.

Alisa pulled out her phone and made a call.

7

Zora jerked awake and sat up in bed. Her heart beat loudly in her chest, her dark hair plastered around her face, and her night clothes drenched in cold sweat. She took deep breaths to calm herself, saying Psalm Twenty-Three over and over again till her heart rate slowed to normal.

She'd had a nightmare again. This time, she couldn't remember the details. All she knew was feeling like she was being suffocated, similar to her ordeal at the detention center when her cellmate had tried to kill her. The memories seemed to come flooding back at night, even though Zora could keep them at bay during the day.

Zora swept the stray hair strands away from her face and ran her hands over the top of her head. Her body ached. Zora couldn't remember when she'd last had a decent night's sleep, and it was telling on her.

She sighed. Zora didn't deserve any of this. It was only because the bad guys thought she was easy prey, someone they could kidnap or throw into jail whenever they wanted. She was so tired of being targeted. Zora couldn't undo the ordeal she'd been through, but it was time she mastered a way to protect herself.

She checked the time. It was a few minutes past midnight. He'd told her she could call at any time, so she picked up her phone and did that.

Thirty minutes later, Zora stood next to Lieutenant Dave McKesson, her boyfriend and a detective with the local PD, inside a private boxing gym. Dave had called Zora a few hours ago to let her know they'd promoted him from detective to lieutenant to replace his corrupt boss, who had played a role in Zora's arrest. She felt bad about waking him from sleep. But boxing had been the first thing to come to her mind, and it was part of Dave's workout routines.

"Are you sure about this?" Dave asked. "We both know how important your hands are for your work."

"I am," Zora responded. "It's not like I'm going to compete with anyone." Martial arts would have been a better skill to learn, but Zora needed an outlet right now to work out her frustrations, so boxing was it. "Sorry about waking you so early."

"No problem."

Zora checked out the expansive space. It was a modern whitewashed studio, boasting polished hardwood floors with a dedicated wall lined with rows of hook racks for boxing gloves above a cubby hole storage unit filled with gym supplies, a huge contrast to the poster-filled decor of boxing greats she'd expected. A professional-sized boxing ring stood in the center of the space, surrounded by four heavy bags hanging from exposed steel beams like sentries. *Nice.* "Is this your gym?" she asked.

Dave laughed. "I wish. It belongs to a friend of mine for his private workouts, but I have an access card for the place."

Zora smiled back. "Okay."

"Shall we?" Dave led Zora to a corner of the gym where one of the heavy bags hung. Zora dropped her gym bag on a nearby small bench and pulled off her hoodie, leaving on a sports bra and a pair of yoga pants.

Dave walked over to the supplies wall and picked up hand wraps and a pair of gloves. "Why don't we start with this?" he said as he strolled back to where she stood. "Just watch me do it. I'm pretty sure you can replicate this next time." He proceeded to wrap both her hands.

Zora could tell that he'd done this many times, given the speed and precision with which he applied them. Then he slipped the gloves over her hands.

"These look different from the usual ones I've seen," Zora said.

"They are molded bag gloves," Dave responded. "Perfect for your delicate hands."

Zora snorted and bit back her laughter.

"What?" Dave asked, a teasing smile on his lips. "They're delicate, aren't they?"

"Oh, please."

Dave grinned and then turned serious. "Okay, why don't we start with your stance and then go from there?"

"Sounds good to me."

"Since you're right-handed, you'll stand with your left foot forward and your right leg back about a shoulder width apart on the center line. Make sure you distribute your weight evenly across both legs. Bend your knees a little. That's it. Keep your right hand in the back with your elbows down and your hands up. Good. Make sure your head is behind your gloves, your chin slightly down, and you can see over the gloves. Great. Then relax and breathe. You're doing great."

"It doesn't seem that hard," Zora said.

"Wait until you have to maintain this stance all the time. I'm sure you'll get the hang of it."

"Okay, what's next?"

"Now we need to work on your footwork." Dave took Zora through how to step with the lead foot and drag with the rear foot and how that would change depending on what direction she wanted to move. It was actually fun, unlike what she'd expected. Then he showed her how to throw a punch, which she practiced on the heavy bag.

"You seem to have gotten the hang of it," Dave said. "With a couple more practices, you might be a good sparring partner."

Zora chuckled. "No, thanks. I'll stick to the inanimate objects like this one." Zora patted the heavy bag. "Would it be okay if I practiced alone for some time?"

"Sure, here's the access card." Dave extended it to Zora. "You can lock up once you're done."

Zora accepted the card. "Are you sure you won't need it soon?"

"I got permission from my friend to give you a

copy. You can use it to come here whenever you want."

Zora beamed at him. Trust Dave to think ahead. "Thank you."

"Just make sure you don't stay too long. This is your first time, and we want to be careful with those delicate hands."

Zora laughed. "What's with you and these hands, anyway? I promise I won't stay too long."

"Okay." Dave's eyes searched hers. "You weren't able to sleep?" Zora nodded. "It gets easier over time, even if the nightmares don't go completely away."

That was good to know. "Thanks, Dave."

"I'll see you later," Dave said as he patted her shoulder.

Zora started punching the bag again, and soon the creak of the door let her know he had left.

She stopped and sighed. It wasn't Dave's fault that Marcus had died, but somehow she'd found it hard to concentrate on their relationship. Things had cooled between them since the incident. It was like a little wall had sprung up between them, and Zora didn't have the energy to tear it down. Her tendency had been to withdraw like she'd done with him when her sister had disappeared, but Dave wasn't letting her go this time around. He'd been patient about everything, showing up as her friend, and giving her the space she needed.

Zora started punching the bag again. Why did she have to go through this ordeal? She threw another punch. All she wanted was to work as a surgeon, help patients, and live a good life surrounded by friends and family. Another punch. And why did Marcus have to die? A double punch. Zora punched the bag harder and harder as she thought about all she'd gone through, until she had to force herself to stop and hug the heavy bag. If she continued, she might hurt her hands, which she needed for the surgeries she would restart this week. By now, she was sweating a lot, and her chest heaved with the effort of taking each breath.

She would get stronger, and she would have the life she wanted. It didn't matter what had happened, the nightmares that remained, or the dear friend Zora had lost. She would overcome any obstacles and get the life she wanted, the one she deserved. And best of all, she would find her sister.

Nothing and no one was going to stand in her way.

8

The man's torso jerked as the defibrillator paddles connected with his chest, but the endotracheal tube remained in place.

"Still in pulseless V-tach!" the nurse called out.

"Another milligram of epinephrine IV, then shock again at one-twenty," the resident ordered as the attending arrived at the scene.

The epinephrine slid through the central line, and the torso jerked again at another shock of the paddles. A second nurse continued pumping the chest, while a third took notes.

"What do we have here?" the attending asked, reaching for the ECG recording.

"Sean Connelly, a fifty-five-year-old male who

arrived three minutes ago in pulseless V-tach. Paramedics said his neighbor found him slumped in front of his apartment. They began CPR and continued for about fifteen minutes until they arrived here. Wife is out of town but is on her way back. He's already had a couple doses of epinephrine en-route. Patient arrived unconscious to the ER. Pupils are equal and reactive, lungs are clear, and abdomen is normal with bowel sounds. BP is sixty over thirty. Oh, and the patient was just discharged yesterday from this ER."

The attending glanced sharply at the resident. "For what?"

"Arrived with gastric pain; diagnosed with gastric ulcer with H-pylori infection, and placed on omeprazole, amoxicillin, and clarithromycin."

"Any known allergies?"

"None from his records."

Then the attending read the ECG recording, and his eyes widened. "What about the bloodwork?"

"We're still waiting for the results," the resident responded as the CPR continued.

"We need it ASAP. Let's get someone on it," the attending said. The resident motioned to the intern, who left to take care of it. "Do we have digoxin on the medication list?"

"No, only the three drugs I've mentioned," the resident replied.

"Let's give this patient 400 milligrams of digoxin-immune Fab IV over five minutes." A nurse rushed to administer the order.

Then the first nurse rechecked the pulse. "No pulse. Still in V-tach!" she called out.

"Amiodarone 300 milligrams IV," the attending ordered as he quickly examined the patient. The drug slid through the line as CPR continued.

The tension mounted in the room, most eyes on the monitor's screen.

But the rhythm continued in v-tach and then flatlined.

"We have asystole!" the nurse checking shouted.

"Another milligram of epinephrine IV," the attending called out.

A nurse administered the dose, but despite that, the flatline remained steady.

The tension in the room rose to another level.

The intern arrived with a tablet and handed it to the attending, who scanned the results. "Just what I thought. Digoxin toxicity with hyperkalemia."

The nurse continued CPR for the next thirty minutes, the tension in the room so thick one could cut it with a knife. They continued to check the rhythm and pulse every two minutes and administered epinephrine every four minutes, yet there was no change.

But it was not over yet; this was a race to save a life. "Let's give another dose of 400 milligrams of digoxin-immune Fab IV over five minutes," the attending ordered.

A nurse delivered the dose, and all eyes watched as the CPR continued for another thirty minutes, each compression as consistent as the last.

Then the attending turned to the nurse in charge of the CPR. "Stop CPR," he said. He listened to the patient's lungs and heart with the stethoscope, checked the central pulse, pupillary response, and motor reaction to pain. There was no respiratory effort, audible breath sounds, heart sounds, or palpable pulse. His pupils were fixed, dilated, unresponsive to light, and there was no motor response to stimulus. The attending checked the monitor—asystole. Doppler showed no blood flow and no cardiac motion. Then he straightened. "Has his wife or any other next of kin arrived?"

The intern rushed out and then came back. "No," he said.

The attending looked around at the other medical

staff for confirmation. "I believe additional heroic measures are futile, and I'm ready to call the code. Are we all in agreement?" Everyone echoed their assent. It was time.

"Okay," he said. "Time of death is 7:05 AM."

9

Andy read the alert on his phone. The man was dead—he should have been grateful that Andy had let him off easy compared to the crimes he'd committed. Anyone who messed with helpless young women deserved to rot in hell. Even worse for what they'd done to Sammy.

His jaw muscle twitched and his nostrils flared as he remembered seeing her lying there, broken, a mere shadow of the bright young woman she'd been. Andy took a series of breaths to calm himself and forced thoughts of her away. He wouldn't grieve. No, not until all those responsible were dead.

Andy got up from the lone chair in the room. It was time to take care of the next person on the list. He'd heard rumors that a hospital committee was poking around, close to what he'd set up. But he wasn't worried—they would find nothing. Still, he planned to keep a close eye on them.

For now, he had an appointment to make.

Seventeen down, three more to go.

10

Andy opened the door of the bar and entered. The bar's run-down exterior contrasted with its clean nineteen-fifties interior decor of black and turquoise checkered vinyl flooring, light brown wood wall paneling, and dark brown furnishings. A gramophone belted out soft oldies music from a corner of the room.

A few patrons sat in high-backed, vinyl-cushioned seats paired around the tables. The place looked sleepy, idyllic even, but Andy knew that would change once evening came, when only those Orsville's chosen few had accepted could enter the bar, wives excluded.

He strode to the long bar that ran the length of the room and sat down. He'd come here often enough during the day that he only attracted the occasional glance.

Andy waited until the bartender approached him. "What would you like to drink?" the woman asked.

"Only a glass of water," Andy answered.

The woman nodded and soon returned with a glass of water garnished with a slice of lemon. She slid the glass in front of him.

Andy pulled a ten-dollar bill from his pocket and slipped it with a tiny sheet of paper to her in return. The woman collected both and stuffed it into her apron.

Andy nursed his drink for a few minutes and then downed it in one go, got up, and left.

The plan was now in motion.

Number eighteen, primed for death.

ora tucked her car keys into her medical coat pocket and strode into the hospital. It felt good to be back. She had missed being a part of this place. Sure, she'd been here last week to help with the mayor's daughter's case, but that had only been on an interim basis. Hopefully, nothing else would happen this time around to take her away from this place.

Zora entered the elevators and exited on the fourth floor. She got the occasional look from the staff and patients mingling on the floor, but nothing more. Zora let out a sigh of relief. She was thankful for that, at least.

Soon she entered the surgery department chair's office. His secretary, Julie, sat as usual at her desk in the front office. She flashed Zora a brief smile. "You may go in," she said. "He's expecting you."

Zora nodded in return and knocked at the door to the inner office.

"Come in," a faint voice said.

Zora stepped into the large office. Even though she'd been here last week, she still couldn't believe how much the office had changed since Dr. Thompson took over from his predecessor, who'd had to resign for the role he played in Zora's last case. Everything in the office was in its spot that she wondered if Dr. Thompson had obsessive-compulsive disorder. But Zora could now see the dark blue carpeting on the floor.

The bespectacled surgeon looked up from where he sat reading behind his maple desk and gestured at her to take a seat in a visitors' chair. "Welcome back," Dr. Thompson said as Zora sank into the chair.

"Thank you," Zora responded. So no welcoming smile. Well, she couldn't say she was surprised, though it would have been nice to receive one for a change. After all, one of their very own had resigned, and another had died because of her involvement. It would probably get worse in the next few days as she got reintegrated back into the system.

He laid the papers he'd been reading back on his

desk and steepled his fingers. "Dr. Smyth, as discussed with your lawyers, you'll be back in your role as chief surgical resident and have the chance to finish up your residency," he said. "Your schedule would also be back to normal, but…"

Zora fisted her hand on her lap. But what? What new thing had they cooked up? Of course, they must be upset that her lawyer, AKA Mom, had practically threatened the hospital to ensure Zora's return to her post. Maybe this was their payback.

"We have a new assignment for you besides your previous responsibilities," Dr. Thompson continued.

Zora's heart thumped with dread. This was code for 'we've found a role for you that no one else wants to take.' How bad was it?

"Given how much attention you've had from the media, we figured it might be good to get you away from the spotlight, and we decided a role on the medical reconciliation committee might be good for you instead. It's a new oversight committee that has only met twice since its creation. You'll be representing the surgery department on the committee," he finished.

Yikes. Like that was related in any way. She was being sent to the dungeon. They most likely just wanted to piggyback on her publicity to show they cared about patient safety. She was pretty sure the hospital's ratings had gone down since the organ trafficking case broke, and they wanted to boost their ratings while punishing her at the same time.

Yes, medical reconciliation work was a priority for the hospital in ensuring patient safety, and it was critical for ensuring patients didn't end up with preventable adverse drug events. But all the physicians she knew hated it. It was an additional workload on top of an already intense work schedule, and no doctor wanted any part of it, as it tended to slow down patient care. The hospital had been making recent efforts to incorporate medication reconciliation into the admissions and discharge workflows, and the medical staff had been resisting the program. So why would they plug her into it if it wasn't some kind of punishment? She already had most of the staff hating her. Did they have to make it worse? She couldn't accept this.

"But what about my existing workload?" Zora asked. "There's no way I can fit this committee work into it! And isn't this work reserved for attendings?"

Dr. Thompson raised an eyebrow at her. "Aren't you planning to apply for a fellowship spot here?"

Thank you, Dr. Thompson. Yes, I know a fellow ultimately becomes an attending. Way to use my dream against me. "Still, the work would be too much for me, and this is my last year of residency. I need to make it count."

Dr. Thompson leaned back. "Exactly! The medical reconciliation role would do just that. No other resident would have it on their resume and application for fellowship. I'm only seeing the upsides here."

From the stern look on his face, Zora gathered that Dr. Thompson was ready to argue with her till she was blue in the face, which meant the hospital leadership had made up their minds about this, and it was no use fighting their decision. She was sure they hoped to stash her there till they decided she could cause them no further troubles.

"Don't worry, Dr. Smyth," Dr. Thompson continued. "You'll still have time for your surgeries, though we've made a *tiny* change to your schedule."

Zora felt her shoulders sag. Right. More like a lot. Lexinbridge Regional was notorious for its time-consuming committees. There was no way it would be different in this case.

"Julie will give you your new schedule on your way out. I'll be expecting regular updates from you on this. And did I mention your first committee meeting will be starting..." he checked his watch, "... in about five minutes?"

Zora jumped to her feet. Five minutes? Dr. Thompson must really hate her to have scheduled this chat with her so close to the medical reconciliation meeting time. That wasn't enough time to get to any other conference room that wasn't in this hospital wing! Arriving late was a poor way to introduce herself on the first day.

"The venue is in the packet Julie will give you," Dr. Thompson said.

She raced out of the inner office without bothering to say goodbye. Julie was ready with the packet as Zora flew out. "Here you go," Julie said. "It's in B101."

The basement conference room. Zora flashed a smile of gratitude as she accepted the envelope and raced out of the outer office. She didn't even notice if people were looking at her or not, as she hastened to the conference room.

There was no time to examine the packet and checkout her new schedule.

Zora just needed to get to the meeting on time.

All conversation ceased and ten pairs of eyes focused on her as soon as Zora stepped into the conference room. Zora shivered from a sudden chill that was not from the room's temperature. It was a minor miracle that she'd made it on time.

She pasted a small smile on her face and grabbed the only seat that was available toward the back of the room between a buxom middle-aged lady with pink glasses, whom she guessed was a director of nursing, and a young man in business casual whose thick eyebrows would be perfect for a facial makeover.

"Welcome, Dr. Smyth," said the presenter, who sat at the head of the table, and whose lab coat indicated he was a pharmacist.

So much for coming in incognito. "Thank you," Zora responded.

"I'm not sure how much you know about this committee, but the hospital leadership pulled it together to oversee a monthly review of all medical reconciliations completed for patients we've deemed at the highest risk of preventable adverse drug events: those who either take medicines with a high risk of harm if used incorrectly, consume multiple medications for different diseases and conditions, or who are going through transitions of care.

"The aim is to pinpoint and correct issues in the medical reconciliation workflow as well as identify any potential drug events and correct them before they happen. This committee is also responsible for investigating any preventable adverse drug event. Why don't I introduce myself, and then everyone can do the same?" the pharmacist said. "I'm Terry Clarke, an assistant director of pharmacy here at Lexinbridge Regional, and the head of this committee on behalf of..."

Zora listened as each member seated around the table introduced themselves. There were representatives from the nursing administration, medicine, pediatrics, ob-gyn, physical rehabilitation, patient safety, and some other groups. Zora didn't catch most of their names, but she would commit them to memory in time.

"Thank you, everyone," Terry said once the introductions were done. "I'm assuming we've all received the information packet via email. Dr. Smyth, here's a physical copy, since you didn't get one." Terry handed a document to Zora. "So why don't we jump in and discuss the results from last month's medical reconciliation?"

Zora scanned the papers in her hands. They'd stripped off all patient identifying information, as expected. Listening to Terry as he walked them through the analyses in the report reminded Zora how important the patient's medical history was when first seen in the ER. Since she wasn't well-versed in the nitty gritty of medical reconciliation, Zora decided that was going to change, which meant lots of reading over the next few days.

She flipped through the documents in her hand again, and a table on the third page that listed details on the potential and preventable adverse drug events for the last six months caught her eye.

Zora studied the information. A high percentage of the cases, more than for any other town, were from the nearby town of Orsville. A closer look showed that over eighty percent of the Orsville deaths were from patients that were not considered high risk for adverse events.

This is strange. It shouldn't have been the case.

"Does anyone have questions about the results?" Terry asked. Apparently, he'd come to the end of his presentation, and Zora hadn't noticed.

"I do," Zora said. All eyes turned in her direction. "Is there any reason why most of these cases are from Orsville?"

Terry gave her a patronizing smile. "It's a town close to us, and since we have the best health facilities in the area, we would expect them to end up here."

"But there are other towns close to us as well, and their numbers are not significant. Why would Orsville be different? What's even stranger is Orsville has a much higher rate of preventable adverse drug events that end up in death than in any other town, and most of those deaths are from patients who were never at high risk for an adverse drug event."

Terry pursed his lips. "So, what are you saying?"

"I think we need to probe deeper into why that's the case. Maybe there's something there that we can resolve that would help minimize the preventable adverse drug events."

Terry crossed his hands over his chest. "I'm not sure if there's any reason to go to that level of analysis. Orsville is the largest town closest to Lexinbridge, so I think the numbers make sense for them."

"Even when their numbers are more than Lexinbridge, which is way bigger than Orsville?" Zora countered. "I don't think doing the analysis would hurt."

A knock sounded on the door and a young lady with a ponytail poked her head in. Terry gestured at her to come in. The lady strode over and whispered something in Terry's ear.

Terry looked at her sharply. "Are you sure?"

"Yes," the lady said, and handed Terry a document.

"What is it?" the nurse administration lady asked.

Terry cleared his throat. "We just had another case of a preventable adverse drug event."

"How's the patient doing?" This was from the young man sitting at her side.

"The patient just passed away," Terry replied.

"Where's the patient from?" Zora asked.

Terry flipped through the document in his hand.

Then he looked up in surprise. "From Orsville."

———

Soon, the meeting ended, and the group dispersed. The committee agreed the Orsville angle needed to be explored and voted that Zora should join Terry in investigating it, with the two providing an update to the committee in an impromptu meeting slated for next week. Zora wasn't keen on being involved in any investigation and only wanted to maintain a low profile, but a patient who shouldn't have been dead had passed away, and she couldn't ignore that. So she agreed to do it. After all, it wouldn't be risky, right?

Zora got up and headed toward the door. As she exited the conference room, someone bumped into her.

She stumbled, and her bag dropped to the floor. Zora bent down to pick it up, but a hand reached down, grabbed it before she had a chance, and offered it to her. "I'm so sorry," he said.

Zora straightened and accepted the bag. The clean-shaven young man standing in front of her looked to be in his early thirties and could have passed for a GQ model if he hadn't been wearing scrubs. Zora could see from his badge that he was a patient care assistant. A turquoise cat pendant hung from a black braided cord around his neck. Was that a black smudge on the cat's nose? The young man noticed where she was staring at and tucked the pendant out of view. Then he turned and rolled a wheelchair away as he left.

Zora stared after him. What was he doing here? This section of the basement had no patient care services... well, except for the small radiology lab located a few doors away. Maybe the young man had dropped off a patient there.

She frowned. But the surgery department used

that radiology lab, and Zora had never seen his face before, either on the wards or in the ER.

"He was just transferred from Medicine," a female voice said behind her. Zora turned to see the physician representing the internal medicine department standing behind her. "He's great eye candy, but he hasn't let it go to his head and is always courteous to the patients and other medical staff. Everyone misses him," the doctor said in a wistful tone. "Surgery is lucky to have him."

Zora watched as the young man continued down the hallway. Maybe he would serve as a distraction for the medical staff on her floor, which would turn their attention away from her, granting her some peace from being the focus of the hospital's rumor mill.

Then Terry joined her at her side. "I'm ready," he said.

It was time to head down to the ER and investigate the adverse drug event case. Zora hoped it was a simple one.

But she couldn't shake off the feeling there was more to it than met the eye.

Zora arrived at the ER cubicle. Luckily, they hadn't moved the body to the morgue yet. She pulled back the sheet that covered his face—he looked like he was just sleeping; rigor hadn't set in yet.

Terry joined her then; he'd stopped to check in with the nurses, as was his usual routine for any preventable adverse drug event case that happened in the ER.

"Zora, what are you doing here?"

Zora turned to see Cameron Marks, an attending in Medicine who'd been her chief resident when she was a medical student. "Hello, Dr. Marks," Zora said with a smile.

Cameron reached her side. "You know better than to call me that."

Zora chuckled. "Hello, Cameron."

"That's better. I haven't seen you in a while."

"Did you travel?" Zora asked.

"I took some time off to do some pro bono work and just got back a few days ago. How are you?"

"I'm good. Was this your patient?" Zora asked.

"Yes. Did you know him?"

Zora explained what they were there to do. "Did this patient have any history of heart problems?"

Cameron shook his head. "None that was documented. That was what was so strange about the digoxin toxicity. No prior history, and his heart seemed fine when on his last visit to the ER. No previous digoxin prescriptions."

"Do you think he was suicidal?"

"I'm not sure, but nothing points to that. No one noticed any signs while he was in the ER on his last visit, and even his wife insists he wasn't since he was still making plans for the holidays with her. He received a promotion a few days ago in the office, and he was happy about that."

"Did we ever receive any of his records from his primary care physician?"

"Our systems aren't connected with those of the Orsville health network, so we had to request a copy of his records by fax. They arrived after his demise, but there was no history of any heart condition or digoxin prescription."

So this was a patient who'd had no heart problems, received no digoxin prescriptions, and most likely hadn't planned to commit suicide by drug overdose, who suddenly appeared in the ER with levels of digoxin in his system, high enough to kill him. Unfortunately, he'd ingested clarithromycin, which has a known interaction with digoxin, further worsening its levels. If he hadn't ingested the digoxin intentionally, then it must have gotten into his system some other way.

"What about his wife?" Zora asked.

"I would assume she'd gone to make some arrangements. Unfortunately, she arrived after he'd passed on." Cameron glanced at his watch. "Listen, Zora, I have to go."

"Okay."

"It's good to see you. We should catch up some other time."

So he hadn't heard about what happened to Zora—there was no way he'd want to interact with her if he'd known. Zora gave him a small smile. "Same here," she responded. Then Cameron left.

"We need to talk with the wife," Terry said.

Zora started. She'd forgotten he was here. "You scared me," she said.

Terry chuckled. "Sorry."

"Hello, who are you?"

Zora turned to see a stylish, slim, middle-aged woman with a short bob hair style. "Are you Mrs. Connelly?"

"Yes. What are you doing in this room?" she asked in a cautious tone.

"I'm so sorry for your loss," Zora said.

Mrs. Connelly's shoulders slumped. "Thank you."

"Mrs. Connelly, we just wanted to ask you a few questions about what happened to your husband," Terry said. "It's something we do in the hospital when we have a death in the ER."

Mrs. Connelly studied their badges and then she said, "Go ahead."

"Was he ever prescribed any digoxin?" Zora asked.

Mrs. Connelly shook her head. "This was my first time hearing about the drug. I usually read up on the internet any drugs the doctors prescribe us, and it doesn't sound familiar."

"Did anything happen to him of late?"

"Nothing out of the ordinary." She thought for a moment. "Except a few months ago when he started feeling tired and lost his appetite, which was a big deal if you knew Sean." Tears came to her eyes, and she brushed them away. Zora waited for her to compose herself. "Then he felt fine again," Mrs Connelly continued. "It would come and go, and we just thought it wasn't a big deal. Oh, there was a day he even complained his vision was yellow, and then it cleared. We laughed about it since it was so weird."

The symptoms sounded like the beginning signs

of digoxin toxicity. "Did you tell the ER doctor about these symptoms?"

"I thought we did, but I'm not so sure anymore."

Zora was pretty sure the patient's notes had listed none of that. The ER resident who saw him the first time would have written them down if they'd told him. So, it seemed more likely that either the Connellys had forgotten to mention them or had intentionally held back from telling the doctor about the symptoms as patients were sometimes known to do. If the information had been in the patient notes, the attending would have seen it during his review and insisted on blood work to check for digoxin, which would most likely have saved Mr. Connelly's life.

"Everything was great again for a while," Mrs. Connelly continued. "We were so happy. He'd gotten a promotion, and things were going well. But then he started having stomach pains, and I rushed him to the ER. He was almost back to his normal self by the time they discharged him, so when I needed to travel out of town for a family emergency as soon as we got home from the ER, I figured he'd be fine by himself. I was supposed to come back later tonight. If only I had known that... I should have stayed home..."

Mrs. Connelly's voice cracked, and she shook with silent sobs.

"Do you have anyone to stay with you?" Zora asked gently.

Mrs. Connelly wiped her tears with a handkerchief that she'd produced from her bag. "My sister is on her way now."

"We'll stay with you till she gets here," Zora said.

Mrs. Connelly gave her a grateful smile. "Thank you."

With the symptoms Mr. Connelly had been having, it was possible he'd been ingesting digoxin for a while. If he wasn't taking it voluntarily, then someone was getting it into his system without his knowledge, which meant someone had wanted him hurt or dead. Did this mean this was most likely a murder case?

Zora's heart sank. This was the last thing she needed.

If the other Orsville deaths turned out to be similar, then this was much bigger than her, and Zora wanted no part of it.

Alisa leaned back in her swivel chair and closed her eyes. Finally, a much-deserved break after a hectic morning. She'd spent her first few hours at work dealing with complaints regarding one of the family's companies. The employees from the garbage hauling business had accused their manager, Eduard, of stiffing them of their weekly pay. Eduard had threatened the employees to keep them quiet, but that hadn't worked, and the case had reached the ears of Alisa and her father.

Unfortunately, the family had strict rules about touching the company funds, so one of her father's trusted men was going to deal with the problem, which meant Eduard might not see the light of day again. There was nothing she could do to stop it, as much as Alisa hated how the problem was going to be solved.

Alisa mentally shook her head. She didn't have the luxury to dwell on the case. Alisa still had piles of contracts to review regarding the existing construction, cement manufacturing, and restaurant businesses, and new investment plans to develop concerning the technology industry. It exhausted her just thinking about it all. Yet, in the back of her mind, she couldn't forget the picture she'd found in Stewart's room.

There was a knock on her door, and her right-hand man, Pete, walked in. Alisa had met Pete in the first year of law school in Boston after Alisa saved Pete from getting mugged on his way home late one night during exams. They had become fast friends and stayed that way till the end of law school. Pete had followed her and worked with her ever since, after Alisa had returned to Lexinbridge to manage the family's legitimate business. Handsome in a boyish way and clad in a three-piece suit without the jacket, Pete might have seemed carefree, but his persona hid a keen, intelligent mind.

He strode across the room and flopped into the nearest chair facing Alisa's.

"What do you have for me?" Alisa asked.

"Alisa, we've known each other a long time, and you know I'm always on your side no matter what you do. But this time, I think you should stop probing into your brother's death."

Alisa leaned forward. "What did you find, Pete?"

Pete stroked his chin. "I think you should let the dust settle on this one."

Alisa rubbed her forehead. Pete could be frustrating sometimes. He should have known she wouldn't change her mind. "Did you look into Dr. Zora Smyth?"

Pete let out a sigh. He pulled out his phone, tapped the surface, and loud rock music filled the office. Then he leaned forward. "She was at the epicenter of it all. Dr. Smyth was the one who blew the whistle on your brother's organ-trafficking business."

Alisa's heart skipped a beat, and her stomach recoiled at the thought. She'd known her brother did terrible stuff—as most members of crime families did—but her family had been cleaning up their act over the past few years. Organ trafficking? That was a whole other level.

"See what I mean?" Pete said. "And that's not even the worst of it. There were rumors he had all these predatory contracts that caused victims to lose their organs and even their lives. That he even had an incinerator at his office to burn his victims' bodies after he was done with them. Your brother was involved in some really nasty business. But all this is speculation," he whispered.

Bile rose in the back of Alisa's throat, and she shuddered. If it was all true, then Stewart was a serial killer. What would make him go to such lengths? Her family had enough money to take care of them for over three lifetimes. No, there was no way he was involved in something so gruesome. There had to be some other hidden truth she still needed to unearth. "So, how did Dr. Smyth get mixed up in his business?"

"Two of her comatose patients had missing kidneys, and she tried to find out what had happened. She tied the case back to her mentor at the hospital, a doctor they caught with one of your father's men at a place where they held her captive. Some are saying your brother offed the mentor to stop him from spilling secrets and then had a hand in getting Dr. Smyth arrested for the murder of her mentor, while others whisper your father was involved."

Alisa stared at Pete in horror. "Are you saying my father must have known about it?"

Pete looked around before answering. "I think we should stop here. Like I said, everything is speculation."

Alisa collapsed back in her swivel chair. Organ trafficking, kidnapping, and murder. If her family was still involved in all these activities, had the reform been all an act? Was this why her father hadn't wanted her to dig into this case? Even if the truth hurt and scarred her, she had to find out everything. "But who killed my brother? Was it Dr. Smyth?"

"Word on the street is that Uncle Jimmy's gang offed your brother. It's said that your brother ordered a hit on one of Dr. Smyth's friend who was investigating the case, and it turned out he was Uncle Jimmy's nephew."

"Crap." So Stewart's death was a revenge killing? Justice wasn't even pertinent here if everything she'd heard so far was true.

"Indeed. It wasn't public knowledge, but I doubt your brother didn't know about their relationship. Also…"

Alisa's heart thudded. There was more? "What? Spit it out already."

"I heard your brother might have had a crush on Dr. Smyth."

That would account for why he had a well-worn

picture of her. But wait? "He sent his crush to jail?" That was as twisted as it got.

"Let's just say your brother had a complex mind. So now that you have the general idea about what happened, what are you going to do about it?"

Alisa rubbed her face. All this new information was making her head spin, and she couldn't even separate the truth from the lies. Had the family she'd known only been a figment of her imagination? "I don't know," she said. "Sometimes I wish…"

"What? That none of this existed?"

"That I was born into a normal family, you know."

Pete scoffed. "Normal is overrated, though I would say your family pushes the limit."

Alisa heard the bitterness in Pete's voice. He never talked about his family, but Alisa knew there was a story there, one he didn't wish to remember.

"But as your friend," Pete continued, "I would advise you to abide by your father's wishes and forget about all this. Have you forgotten how horrible Stewart was to you? Just focus on living your own life."

What Pete said made sense. Stewart was dead, and Alisa still needed to live, even if everything about her family had been smoke and mirrors, something she refused to believe.

But living her own life? "I'm not sure that's possible anymore," she said.

"Are you just going to give up?"

She knew what Pete was referring to. She'd long had a secret dream of leaving the country and everything else behind. But how could she do that when she was now the only person her father had? As much as she craved her independence away from the family and its crime-related activities, family was still everything to her. She couldn't just turn her back on her father when he needed her.

But something told her things would never be the same again.

13

"I want no part of it," Zora said to Dr. Thompson as she sat across from him in his office.

"What are you talking about, Dr. Smyth?"

"The medical reconciliation committee."

Dr. Thompson fiddled with the pen he'd been writing with when she entered. "What do you mean? I thought we'd already discussed this."

"I know, and I just thought it would be a simple case of hospital policy and helping to make it better. But potential murder cases? I didn't sign up for that."

Dr. Thompson's hand stilled. "What are you talking about?"

"Sean Connelly, the patient who died from digoxin toxicity? The one I'm sure they've updated you about? I think he was murdered. There was no history of heart problem, digoxin prescription, or suicidal tendencies, and yet it's likely the man received the drug over time without his knowledge. Wouldn't that mean someone else wanted him hurt or dead?"

"This is the first time I'm hearing of this, and there is no evidence to support it. Abandoning the committee would be considered a dereliction of duty, Dr. Smyth. Don't forget the Hippocratic Oath."

Zora jumped to her feet. "Dr. Thompson," she said a little too calmly, "My job is to save lives, not deal with murders, so this is where my involvement with the committee ends. You can handle it as you please."

She walked out of his office without waiting for his response. The hospital couldn't do anything to her for declining the position—she'd read the contract her mother had made the hospital sign.

Zora wasn't going to get involved with this case, and nothing and no one could make her.

14

Zora stretched her neck from side to side as she exited the OR. She was on day call from the schedule Julie had given her, and so far she'd operated on an exploratory laparotomy, a bowel resection, and an emergency appendectomy.

Thankfully, her surgical skills were still top-notch, but that didn't mean she would ever stop working on them. Her hands ached a little from the early morning boxing, but they'd remained steady throughout the surgeries. In the future, she'd massage them after every workout session. Fortunately, she only had a few hours before the night float team would take over, and then she was done for the day.

Her pager beeped, and Zora looked at the screen. Her next patient had already arrived. Time to recharge herself with a bottle of water from her locker in the call room before heading to the ER.

"What do we have here?" Zora asked the senior surgical resident-on-call a few minutes later.

"Eric Sawyer, a forty-five-year-old male, was traveling with his wife when the car swerved and hit the guardrail," the blue-eyed brunette responded. "Patient arrived unconscious in the ER. His wife is also receiving treatment here for her superficial injuries.

"Pupils are equal and reactive. He has a Glasgow coma scale of seven with eye opening and movement in response to pain, but is non-verbal. Lungs are clear, abdomen is normal, and bowel sounds are present. BP is eighty over forty, heart rate is fifty-five beats per minute. No history of any medical conditions or medications. We're suspecting possible trauma to the head, but there are no swellings. We've sent the blood for a full blood workup, and we're expecting the results soon. In the meantime, we've given him atropine 0.5 milligrams IV."

Zora examined the intubated patient to confirm what the resident said. Then she studied the ECG reading. Bradyarrhythmia present. *Wait!* Zora peered closer. Was this what she thought it was? Now all the symptoms together made sense. "Did this patient ever take digoxin?" she asked the resident.

The young doctor shook her head. "I suspected the same when I saw that as well and asked his wife, but she said no. He's taking no drugs. His wife also stated he's been happy of late. They'd been trying to have a child for many years and just found out that his wife was pregnant."

Zora stilled. This was the second previously healthy patient coming in with suspected digoxin toxicity. Zora hoped this wasn't what she was thinking. *No, it couldn't be.*

She cast the thought from her mind. The patient in front of her needed her. "Give me one second," she said.

Zora stepped a few feet away and called the attending on-duty. He was just going into surgery for another patient, gave his consent for her to administer the Fab fragments, and updated the order to reflect that.

She returned to the patient's side. "I need 400 mg of digoxin-immune Fab IV over five minutes into this patient *now*," Zora said. A nurse who'd been standing by the gurney rushed to execute the order. Zora watched as she administered the drug into the patient's central line.

An intern hurried over, holding out a hospital-issued tablet. "We have the results," she said.

Zora accepted the tablet and scanned the screen. Just what she thought, but a minute too late to be used to calculate the Fab fragments' dosage. "This patient has hyperkalemia with a potassium level of 6.7."

"Are we going to give him calcium?" the intern asked.

"Unless you want to kill him." Though there were mixed opinions about intravenous calcium—used in the treatment of hyperkalemia—causing increased myocardial contractions and triggering or worsening arrhythmias in digoxin-toxicity patients, Zora preferred to err on the side of caution. "The Fab fragments should take care of the hyperkalemia."

Zora turned to the resident. "Let's transfer this patient to the SICU and send a consult to Cardiology. He might need a temporary cardiac pacemaker in place to manage the bradyarrhythmia and hypotension." The Surgical Intensive Care Unit provided a high level of intensive care and close monitoring to critically ill surgical and trauma patients.

She couldn't help asking one more question. "Do we know where they were traveling to?"

The resident flipped through the patient's notes. "They were returning to their home in Boston."

Zora's shoulders relaxed. So it wasn't what she was thinking. This was just another random adverse drug event. The alternative would have been scary.

"But... yes, here it is... they were coming from their hometown of Orsville," the resident concluded.

Zora's heart sank. Unfortunately, she'd been right after all. Why did she have to be the one to see this patient?

She sighed. "I'll be right back," she said to the resident. "Page me if anything changes before I return."

The resident nodded and then turned and rattled off some instructions to the intern.

Zora left the cubicle and exited the ER.

She had no other choice than to make the call.

"Dr. Smyth, what's going on?" Dr. Thompson asked from the other end of the line.

Zora had to tell him. "We have another digoxin toxicity case. Not listed on his medication history and unlikely to be a suicide attempt since his wife just got pregnant after many years of trying." Zora then gave him additional details about the case.

"It could just be a coincidence," Dr. Thompson said.

"Except they were both from Orsville."

Dr. Thompson went silent for a moment. "Okay, I'll take care of it. Thanks for letting me know. Anything else?"

"That's it."

"Alright. Have a good evening, Dr. Smyth." The line went dead.

Zora leaned against the wall in the hallway that connected the ER to the rest of the hospital. It was out of her hands now, and she wasn't involved in it anymore.

She just needed to make sure it stayed that way.

———

Zora stepped out of the SICU, and the doors closed behind her. Eric Sawyer had improved since they'd administered the Fab fragments. Cardiology had installed a temporary pacemaker, and that seemed to work as well. There was a good chance the patient would make it after all.

Her phone rang. Zora pulled her phone from her

scrubs pocket, looked at the screen, and swiped the answer button. "Hello, Dave."

"Hi, Zora. Are you still in the hospital?"

"Yes, but I'll be leaving once I hand over to the night team. What's up?"

"I just got called in by my captain, who told me he got a call from a lawyer from your hospital about a potential murder case and another attempted murder case that they need us to look into. Your name came up. Seriously, Zora, couldn't you stay away? You don't need this right now."

Zora ran her hand over the side of her hair. "I'm trying to, but these incidents seem to just find me. But telling them about the case is the most I plan to do. I'm not getting more involved. I'm out."

Dave sighed. "I hope it works out that way. You've gone through enough as it is, and we need you to stay safe."

"I agree. Honestly, I just want my normal back."

And Zora was going to get it and make sure it stayed that way no matter what it took.

Andy's face tightened as he stared at the information on his computer screen. A fly buzzed near his ear, and he smacked it away. His new apartment was in the dumps, with mounds of trash that stank to high heaven piled in front of the apartment complex. But the neighborhood gave him the shroud of anonymity he needed—the people who lived here were too caught up in their imaginative worlds to mind any other person's business. Still, he couldn't wait to be out of here.

His mind raced. How had this Dr. Zora Smyth tied the two cases together so quickly? Had he made any mistakes or left any clues behind? Andy didn't think so. Thankfully, he'd been monitoring the new police cases daily and had seen the case information before it got hidden behind multiple layers of security.

Andy frowned. He didn't need anyone snooping around his work. This new development could put a screw in his plans and interfere with his revenge.

The one thing that should never happen.

No one or nothing could stand in his way and derail his mission so close to the end.

Andy cracked his knuckles. It was time to put an end to this investigation before it started.

Zora plopped into a chair at a workstation in a quiet corner of the surgical residents' lounge. She'd gone back to check on Eric Sawyer one more time and then decided to spend the night at the hospital instead. Once she was done with the SICU, she'd showered in the call room before returning to spend the rest of the night in the lounge.

Fortunately, most of the residents were gone for the day; others were in the ER or attending to patients on the wards, which gave her some precious time to herself in the space. It was time to catch up on work—she only had a few months left in her residency program, and she'd lost significant time because of the ordeal she'd been through in the past few weeks. Hopefully, the nightmares would stay away as well.

Zora signed into the computer and reviewed a surgical video recorded during her time away from the hospital. It sucked that she'd missed the chance to watch such a rare surgery, but the replay was better than nothing. Soon she lost track of time as she reviewed and took notes.

Suddenly, the door crashed open, and Herbert the fourth came in as she reached the end of the video.

Her heart sank. Herbert had been one of Graham's lackeys. Graham had been a fellow chief resident who had given Zora a hard time and had been involved in the nasty organ trafficking business. He'd run to Dubai to avoid extradition back to the US. Herbert had hated Zora even before then, though she didn't know why.

"How dare you come here?" Herbert bellowed.

Well, Zora had as much right as any other surgical resident to use the space. "Hello, Herbert."

"We don't allow criminals here," Herbert said with a sneer.

Zora turned back to what she'd been watching. Trying to get through to Herbert was like trying to pour water through a stone. Finishing the video was a better use of her time.

"I'm talking to you, Zora," Herbert said, and grabbed her shoulder.

But Zora was tired of people thinking they could just do anything to her and get away with it. "Get your paws off me," she said in an icy tone. "If you ever touch me again, I'll sue you for harassment and make sure you serve time for it. This is not a warning; it's a promise."

Herbert snatched his hand away as if in surprise. *Yep, Herbert, the Zora of yesterday is gone. You better be careful with this one.* He huffed and puffed and then turned and charged out of the room.

Zora's shoulders slumped. She'd fended off another attack, but how many more would she have to endure until things returned to normal? Zora missed the old her that was happy-go-lucky and didn't have all these terrible memories.

She shook the thought away. She didn't have time for this—Zora still had a lot more work to get through. 'Butt on seat, eyes on screen' was her motto for tonight.

It was all she could accommodate right now.

Zora opened her eyes. She didn't know when she'd moved over to the couch in the residents' lounge and fallen asleep. She already felt refreshed, even though she'd only slept for a few hours. *Oh, no nightmares! Thank you, God!* Maybe she should try spending a couple more nights at the hospital to get some much-needed sleep.

She glanced at her watch—it was almost five a.m. Time to head home and freshen up.

The sound of her ringtone pierced the air, and Zora scrambled to locate her phone. She'd forgotten to put it back on vibrate mode. Zora found it half-buried in a corner of the couch and swiped the answer screen. "Hey, Christina, what's up?"

Christina was Zora's long-time roommate and best friend since high school. She was also a nurse at Lexinbridge Regional and had been kidnapped as well during Zora's last ordeal.

"Zora, you need to come home," Christina said in a shaky voice.

Alarm bells rang in Zora's head, and she sat up. "What's wrong?"

"It's bad, Zora."

Zora rushed into her apartment. "Christina, where are you?" she called out. She'd forgone changing out of her scrubs and was sure her hair was sticking out in all directions.

But it was nothing compared to how her apartment looked. It was like a hurricane had barged through, leaving destruction in its wake, and what wasn't torn up was missing or discarded like a rag doll.

"Over here," Christina said as she came out of her bedroom. The petite redhead had a grim look on her face.

Zora hastened to where she stood and grabbed her arms. "Are you okay?"

Christina gave her a small smile. "I'm fine. Fortunately, I just got in a few minutes ago and wasn't here when it happened. The cops are on their way." Christina was on leave and had gone to visit her mom. She must have returned early. It was a good thing she hadn't been around when this happened.

Zora grimaced. She didn't know which she would have preferred: dealing with the mess herself or involving the cops. Zora had a poor opinion of them as it was, and apart from Dave, she wanted nothing to do with them.

Christina pulled Zora into a hug. "Don't worry. I called Dave, and he's sending one of his trusted colleagues over. We knew you'd want to keep this discreet. It's going to be fine." Her eyes searched Zora's. "But I'm sorry about your room."

Zora stepped out of her arms and rushed toward her room. A hinge had broken, leaving the door ajar, and her room… well, it left Zora speechless. *Okay, calm down, Zora*, she thought. She could get through this. Zora could replace everything, except for one thing.

Please God, let it be there, Zora thought as she sprinted to her closet, pushed the mound of wadded-up clothes aside, and reached into the back of her closet. Her hand connected with a box and she pulled it out.

Zora's heart skipped a beat. *Please God, no*. The shoebox lay crushed and torn up. She pulled it open, and pieces of shredded paper streamed to the floor.

Zora collapsed on the floor. "No!" Why did they have to destroy the letters? They had been mementos from her dad. He'd written notes and letters to Zora almost every week in the last few years of his life, and she'd treasured them. It was one of the few things she had left of him and the most precious.

"Zora…" Christina appeared at the doorway. "Oh, no!" she said when she saw what was in Zora's hands. "I'm so sorry."

"We need to find who did this," Zora said in a bitter tone. Someone had wanted to hurt her, and they'd succeeded.

"There was a note," Christina said. "I haven't touched it since the cops might need it."

Zora's head swung in her direction. "Where is it?"

Zora studied the writing that was splashed in red on her kitchen's accent wall: *STOP WHAT YOU ARE DOING, ZORA. THIS IS YOUR FIRST WARNING.*

The muscle in her jaw twitched. There was only one thing it could be about: the digoxin cases. Someone wanted her to stop looking into them.

Zora gave a harsh chuckle. This was so ironic. She'd done everything to disengage herself from the case, yet the perpetrator had in fact confirmed something fishy was going on and tried to punish her for something she wanted no part of.

Well, she was sick and tired of every psycho on the block thinking they could take a piece of her and get away with it. And her father's letters…

Zora's hand clenched into a fist. She'd had

enough. The only way this would be over was if she solved the case.

If the psycho behind it wanted a fight, that was exactly what they were going to get.

17

Zora pulled her phone and called Dave. "Where are you?" she asked.

"I'm on my way to Orsville. Are you okay?"

She dismissed his concern. "I'm fine. I'd like to come along for the ride."

"Zora, I'm not sure that's a good idea. You should stay out of the case.

"After what just happened?"

"How do you know for sure it's related to the case?"

"Who else could it be?" Dave stayed silent. "See what I mean?" Zora sighed. "The only way I can get my life back is if we solve this case. Let me come with you."

"What about work?"

"I have the day off except for a seminar in the afternoon. I should be back in time for that."

"Alright. I'll be there in five."

"Thanks, Dave. See you soon." Zora ended the call.

Zora turned to Christina. "I'm sorry—"

"Don't worry," Christina said. "I already called Brian, and he's picking me up to take me to your mom's."

Zora raised an eyebrow. "I thought you guys were not speaking to each other." Brian Atkinson was Zora's fellow surgical chief resident and another of her good friends. Christina and Brian had grown close and were always bickering. Zora knew it was because they were fighting their attraction toward each other.

"Brian can be pigheaded sometimes. Zora, what did he expect when he stood me up for dinner? And when I asked him for an explanation, he said he'd tell me later. Then he informs me the next day that he was called in for an emergency surgery. Why couldn't he have just said so? It's not like I wouldn't understand."

Zora chuckled. These two friends of hers. "Do you like him?"

"What do you mean? We're just friends."

"Really?"

Christina blushed. "Zora, you need to get going."

Zora laughed. "Dave's not here yet."

"I'm sure he is," Christina countered. Zora's phone pinged at that moment. "See? I'm certain that's him."

Zora checked her phone screen. Sure enough, it was Dave.

"Go," Christina said. She gave Zora a hug. "I'll see you later. Stay safe."

Zora nodded and left.

Now that she had no choice but to fight back, she had to resolve the case and get her life back to normal as quickly as possible.

***

Zora and Dave stepped out of the primary care physician's office. It turned out Sean Connelly and Eric Sawyer had used the same PCP.

"Well, we learned nothing new," Zora said.

"I agree," Dave said. "But sometimes, it's all about narrowing down the list. Detective work isn't always sexy."

Zora smiled at his words. "So where next?"

Dave looked down at the little notebook in his hands. "The Thirsty Bar."

"The what?"

"I know. I think the name's quirky too. Both wives mentioned the bar when I asked them for their husbands' itinerary for the previous twenty-four hours. There might be something there."

"Okay, let's go," Zora said.

Ten minutes later, Zora and Dave stepped into the establishment. It hadn't been hard to find—the first person they'd asked had provided directions after giving them a weird look.

All conversations halted at their entrance. Dave ignored the change and made his way to the bar. Zora followed, but she could feel the eyes boring into her back. All the patrons were male, and the only female she'd sighted had disappeared.

A buxom woman with a long face approached them as soon as they sat on the bar stools. "We are not open for business," the woman said. But Zora could see they'd attended to the other patrons in the place. So, this was a roundabout way of saying they were not welcome.

Dave flashed his badge. "I'm here on official business. And you are?"

"Laura, the manager," the woman said in a clipped tone.

"Is there anywhere we can talk in private?" he asked.

Laura studied them with cold eyes. Then she said, "Come this way."

She led them around the bar to a tiny office in the back, its wall plastered with old newspaper clippings. Zora guessed these were from the nineteen fifties, which was in sync with the bar's decor. Laura sat behind a battered desk and motioned to a red couch with stains of various colors and sizes. Zora didn't want to think about where those stains might have come from.

"No, thanks," Dave said. "We'll be quick and get out of your hair." He pulled a picture from his jacket and slid it across the desk to the woman. "Do you know this man?"

Laura glanced at the picture without touching it. "Yes, that's Mr. Connelly."

"Is he a regular here?"

"Most folks in this town come here often," she replied. *Good way to deflect without answering the question,* Zora thought.

"Can you remember the last time he was here?" Dave asked.

"Not exactly," she said. "Maybe a few days ago. Too many people coming and going."

"Is there any person in particular you recall seeing him with?"

"Not sure. Too many people." *This lady is keeping all the information close to her chest*, Zora thought.

"How about this guy?" Dave slid a second picture to her.

Laura took the picture and looked at it. "I think he's Eric something. Used to live here and then moved. What about him?"

"Has he been here recently?"

"I think I remember seeing him, but nothing else comes to mind. Is there anything else?"

Dave collected the photos and then slid her a business card. "Thanks for your time. If you remember anything, give me a call." The woman nodded without picking up the business card. "Let's go," Dave said to Zora.

Eyes followed them as they reentered the main bar area and headed to the exit. Soon they stepped out of the bar into the cool air. Zora took a deep breath to expunge the smoky air she'd inhaled in the bar. "That went well," she said. "Did you feel she was hiding something?"

"Possibly," Dave said.

"I think we're back to where we started." Zora looked around. "Does anything strike you as odd?"

Dave's eyes swept the area. "There are fewer people on the street than you'd expect," he said.

"Exactly! And the place looks like a sleepy town from the nineteen fifties instead of the vibrant area it's supposed to be. Now why would that be?"

"That's strange," Dave said.

Someone bumped into Zora, and she stumbled. "Hey! Watch where you're going!" she called out. The person in the hoodie hurried off without looking back.

Dave moved to go after the individual, but Zora grabbed his arm. "It's not worth it," she said. That was when she noticed the note in her other hand. "What's this?"

"Don't open it," Dave said, putting his hand over hers. "Let's look at it once we've left here."

Five minutes later, Dave had finished pumping gas into his car and was back in the driver's seat. "You can open it now," he said.

Zora unfolded the paper, only to see a set of numbers written on it. "That's it?" she asked.

Dave took it from her. "It doesn't look like an account number—not enough digits."

"What could it be for?"

"That's what we have to find out. I'll send it off now for my computer guy to work on it." Dave snapped a picture of the paper with his phone and sent it off with a quick message.

They visited the residences of the victims and some of the other places their spouses had mentioned they frequented but came away empty. Dave also hadn't heard from his computer guy, so they were no closer to understanding what the numbers represented.

They ended up back at the gas station. "What now?" Zora asked.

"I think it's time to leave," Dave said. "I had planned to spend the night, but I'll drive you back and come back later."

"No, I'll just take the train. It's my fault for barging in on your investigation."

Dave gave her a quiet smile. "No, it's fine. I'll drop you off first. I'll get to spend time with my favorite person," Zora's face warmed at that, "and the drive back will give me time to think and maybe shake loose a clue or two I might be overlooking."

"Thank you," Zora said, and leaned back on the headrest.

Just because they'd found little didn't mean it was over.

It was just the beginning, and she planned to see this through.

18

Andy threw the burner phone across the wall, where it fractured and then shattered. The pieces scattered all over the floor.

His chest heaved as he struggled to calm himself. He'd thought Zora would back down from the case; instead he'd fueled her desire to become more involved, and now she'd gone down to Orsville.

"That was such a stupid move," the other man said to Andy. "Now she knows there's definitely someone behind the cases. You gave them a clue, for goodness' sake!"

Andy steepled his fingers. "They still don't know who I am. Don't worry, I have this handled," he told his brother.

His brother sighed and ran his hand through the

hair he insisted was brown, but Andy knew better. It was as blonde as his own, but nothing could change his brother's mind about it. "I hope so. We don't need any problems when we're this close to the end."

"It will be fine. I have it in the bag."

"The woman wants us to stop." Andy knew who his brother was referring to, and it wasn't Zora.

Andy appreciated the help the woman had given all this time, but this was their business, and they wouldn't quit. "That won't happen."

"What are you going to do now?" his brother asked.

"I'm going to get Dr. Smyth to back off. It appears the first warning wasn't enough."

"Just make sure you don't give her any ideas."

"I won't. This will kill two birds with one stone. But I'm going to need your help."

Dr. Smyth would have no choice unless she was just a stubborn fool, and those types didn't last long from what he'd seen.

19

Zora passed through the SICU entrance and soon reached the nurses' station. A tall blonde nurse with freckles sat behind the counter and typed into a computer terminal. She looked up when Zora approached.

The nurse gave her a warm smile. "Dr. Smyth, how are you doing today?"

Did Zora know her? She didn't think so. Zora glanced at her name tag—Angela Langston. "Hello, Nurse Langston. How's the shift going?"

"Great, thanks for asking."

"And how is Eric Sawyer?"

Nurse Langston scanned the board behind her and then turned back to Zora. "He's doing okay. We think he might regain consciousness soon."

"That's great to hear. What about his digoxin and potassium levels?"

"Those have been coming down as well."

This was fantastic news. Eric Sawyer now had a strong chance to live. Zora's efforts to save his life hadn't been in vain. "That's wonderful. I'll just go in and see him." Then Zora saw the man coming out from the cubicle opposite Eric Sawyer's. "What's he doing here?" Zora asked, pointing to the patient care assistant she'd met in the basement.

"You mean Drew Francis?"

That was his name? "Yes."

"He was just assigned to the SICU. He's great with the patients and has been a big help since he started here, and is always willing to assist. I think I've even seen him reading to Eric Sawyer, and we think that might have helped him recover faster. I don't know what we'll do once he leaves for another department. Thankfully, that isn't soon."

"If he's as good as you say, then we need more of him."

Nurse Langston nodded. "Yes, we do."

By now, Zora had lost sight of Drew Francis. *He must have gone into one of the other cubicles*, she thought. She pulled out her phone and checked the time—only a few minutes before she had to be at the seminar. She smiled at Nurse Langston. "Alright, I'll leave you to your work."

"See you later, Dr. Smyth." Nurse Langston turned back to whatever she'd been working on.

Zora bounced down the hallway toward Eric's cubicle. The news of his recovery had put wind in her sails.

Now, he only needed to regain consciousness.

20

Christina poked her head into the kitchen where Zora's mom—Aunt Adrianna to Christina—was cutting up some vegetables. She looked up as the door opened.

"I just got a text from Zora," Christina said. "She wants me to meet her in the SICU."

Aunt Adrianna's eyebrows furrowed in concern. "Is everything okay?"

"I'm sure it is. Maybe there's something she'd like me to do for her." It wasn't an unusual request. Zora and Christina were practically sisters and had asked each other for hundreds of favors over the years.

"Okay, you can take a car parked in front of the

house. The keys are hanging in the coat room off the foyer."

"There's no need, Aunt Adrianna. I already called a car service."

"Fine, but you don't have to do that next time. Use one of the cars whenever you like."

"Thanks, Aunt Adrianna. I'll be back soon."

Christina shut the door and headed out of the house. Her phone pinged—the car service was here.

She hadn't told Aunt Adrianna, but Christina was worried about Zora. The home invasion had rattled Christina, and now Zora had discovered something during her trip to Orsville. What had she found there that she needed to tell Christina in person? She wished all these things would blow over. If anyone deserved peace and a stress-free life, it was Zora.

Christina hurried down the driveway towards the gate where the car service waited.

Time to go see what Zora was up to.

———

Christina headed to the nurses' central station as soon as she entered the SICU. She'd changed into the scrubs from her locker in the nurses' lounge.

Angela, a nurse she'd worked with before, was

on-duty today. *Thank goodness*. It would make it easier for Christina to gain access to the cubicle where Zora was waiting. The hospital had tightened the security protocol for entering patients' cubicles after one of Zora's missing kidney patients, John Doe, had been taken out of the SICU without permission.

"Hey Christina, how are you doing?" Angela asked.

"I'm good. How's the shift going?"

"Not bad. The patients are doing okay, which is all we can hope for. What brings you here?"

"I'm here to see Zora."

"Dr. Smyth? I think I saw her a while ago, but I don't know where she is now."

"She told me which room she was in."

"Okay."

"Can I see her for a few minutes? I'll be quick."

"Fine, but you only have five minutes. After that, I'll come and get you myself if you aren't out."

Christina gave her a smile. "Thank you. I'll see you later."

She grabbed a mask from the box on the counter, spurting and then working some antiseptic into her hands as she headed to the cubicle where Zora was meant to be. Christina passed patients, most of them unconscious and some with medical staff working by their sides, till she arrived at the cubicle she was looking for. She entered and scanned the room.

Where was Zora? The text message had said she'd be here.

That was when she noticed how fast the IV line was dripping. *This is abnormal,* Christina thought. Her eyes jerked to the cardiac monitor, and all she saw was an erratic rhythm racing across the screen.

Shoot! Christina hastened and pressed the code blue button on the wall. The alert would set off the code team's pagers, and the team would be well on their way to the patient before the overhead page's "CODE 9" message followed.

Christina made sure the patient was flat on the bed, removed any pillows, and dropped the head of the bed. She checked the patient's carotid pulse at the neck but found none, so she started compression. Hopefully, it would help before the code team arrived and took over.

Please, don't die on me, Christina prayed as she compressed the patient's chest. This was Zora's patient, and contrary to what most lay folks thought, doctors were affected whenever their patients died. There would be the constant questioning in their minds, as they went through every aspect of care they'd given to the patient and wondered if they had forgotten to do anything, even when it was clearly not the case. Nurses also felt it, but differently—though they were not the final decision makers for patients, they interacted much more closely with them on a day-to-day basis.

The code team arrived with the crash cart and another medical personnel inserted the backboard and took over the compression. Christina stayed in a corner and observed the resuscitation efforts as the team members played their respective roles: the intensivist 'ran' the code, the respiratory therapist managed the patient's airway, a nurse was in charge of the defibrillators, another managed the crash cart and administered IV fluids and medications as ordered by the doctor, while the third nurse documented the entire resuscitation process.

A few other medical and supporting staff, including security, were present to provide their services as needed. Christina was sure another team member had reached out to the patient's family. But where was Zora, anyway? Realizing it was time to leave, Christina made her way toward the cubicle's exit.

A hospital security officer stopped her at the entrance. "Ma'am, are you part of the code team?"

"No," Christina replied. "I came to see this patient's doctor, saw his state, and pressed the code button."

"I have the results," a nurse said as she rushed past Christina into the cubicle. "Severe hyperkalemia."

"Let me see," said the doctor in charge of the code. The nurse handed the result to him. "Unbelievable. How is his potassium level this high? Was this patient placed on potassium for any reason?"

A nurse checked the patient's notes. "None," she said. "His potassium level on the last check twenty minutes ago was 5.5."

The doctor shook his head in bewilderment. "How, for goodness' sake, did this happen?" He glanced at the IV fluid. "Just to be safe, let's change the IV fluid and put up a new one. Make sure you secure the bag removed."

So Christina's instincts had not been wrong about the IV fluid. If the doctor was complaining about the potassium levels being ridiculously high, and the IV drip had been super fast when she'd first seen it, could it be...?

Christina's eyes widened. Attempted murder? It was plausible, since this was one of Zora's digoxin cases under investigation.

Where was Zora, anyway? She'd asked Christina to come, and now she was nowhere to be found. Either way, it was time for Christina to leave. She wanted nothing to do with what was going on and what it could turn into. Christina threaded her way through the security team and headed toward the SICU's main exit.

"Ma'am!"

Christina kept walking. She was certain they couldn't be referring to her, so she just ignored the call.

A muscled hand touched her arm. Christina started and turned. It was the security officer who had spoken to her a few moments ago.

"Ma'am," he said.

"Yes?"

"Could you come with us? We'd like to ask you a few questions about the patient."

Christina's heart thudded. Why? What could she possibly tell them?

"It won't take long," the officer insisted.

Well, she'd done nothing wrong and had nothing to hide. Moreover, she'd saved the patient's life, and they probably just needed to ask her a few questions.

It wouldn't hurt, right?

Zora stepped out from the conference room as soon as the seminar ended. She'd made it in time from the SICU, and the topic had been interesting.

But Zora hadn't been able to concentrate, thinking instead about the digoxin cases. Who was killing off these patients and why? And what did it have to do with Orsville? She was no closer to the answer by the time the seminar concluded, and she'd missed the entire session.

She pulled out her phone to switch it on and saw the multiple missed calls from Christina.

Her heart rate accelerated, and she dialed back Christina's number. There was no response. Zora speed-dialed again, yet it was still the same.

Why wasn't Christina answering her phone? It was abnormal to get that many missed calls from her. Zora hoped nothing was wrong. Then she called Brian's number. He picked up at the first ring.

"Zora," he answered, his voice laden with anxiety.

Zora's heart sank. "What is it, Brian? What's happening with Christina? I just saw her missed calls and dialed her number, but there was no response."

"Christina was just taken to the station."

Zora's heart skipped into a gallop. "For what?"

"For suspicion in the murder of a patient."

"What? What patient?"

"Eric Sawyer."

"What? You're joking, right?" Zora said to Brian. She'd just seen Eric Sawyer before heading into the seminar, and he'd been stable and non-critical. How was it possible? By now, she was running toward the SICU.

"It's true. They are on their way to the station right now. I'm headed there as well."

How was that even possible? Christina had had no dealings with Zora's patient. "Brian, I'll call you back."

Zora speed-dialed Silas' number as she waited for the elevators to arrive. "Hello, Silas."

"Zora, what's happening?" Silas said. "Why do I feel this isn't good news?"

"It's Christina. She's at the local police station."

"I'll take care of it," Silas said without preamble and ended the call.

The elevators still hadn't arrived, so Zora took the stairs till she got to the SICU floor. She sprinted through the doors and raced to the cubicle where Eric Sawyer had been.

"Dr. Smyth, wait!" a nurse called after her, but Zora didn't stop till she entered the cubicle. It was empty, with no evidence anyone had occupied it.

"Dr. Smyth," the nurse said as she caught up with Zora.

It was the same nurse Zora had met earlier. Nurse Langston, if she recalled. "Where is the patient that was here? Eric Sawyer?" she asked.

Zora met her eyes and saw her grim expression. "He's dead. And your friend Christina was here when it happened."

"Why would Christina be here?"

"She said she was looking for you and was supposed to meet you here. We made the mistake of letting her through, and the patient coded soon after she went in."

Christina would never hurt a patient. Something was wrong.

She had to find out the truth, but it was more important to get Christina out first.

———————

Zora stayed out of view outside the police station as she waited for Christina to come out.

She shivered. This place spooked her and brought back flashbacks of her time here. But she had to be here for Christina. Silas had sent her a text that he would get her out soon.

Then Zora saw the figure she'd been waiting for, with Silas in tow, step out from beyond the double sliding doors.

"Christina!" Zora cried, and rushed toward her, pulling her into a hug. "Are you okay?"

Christina looked like a shadow of herself, and Zora understood. Stepping through those doors was an experience she wouldn't wish on anyone. She gave Zora a small smile. "I'm okay," she said.

Zora looped her arm through Christina's. "Let's go home." Then she turned to Silas. "Thanks," she said.

"My pleasure," Silas responded. "Why don't we take my car? Oh, and Brian was here earlier when I arrived, but I told him he could leave since he was still on call at the hospital."

Twenty-minutes later, they arrived in front of Zora's parents' home. Brian had spoken to Christina on their way back and had promised to stop by when his call was over. Zora's mom was waiting outside and rushed forward as soon as she sighted Silas' car.

Silas parked, and Christina stepped out, followed by Zora. Zora's mom grabbed Christina and pulled her into a hug. "I'm so sorry, dear," Zora's mom said.

And that was when the tears came. Christina shook with sobs as Zora's mom held her.

"It's going to be okay, it's going to be okay," Zora's mom said as she patted Christina's back.

Once Christina stopped shaking, Zora's mom wiped away her tears. "Why don't we go inside?" she said.

Zora led the way into the living room, where her mom ensconced Christina on the couch and propped cushioned pillows around her. She had a cup of coffee ready, which she handed over to Christina.

"Thank you," Christina said.

"Oh, it's nothing," Zora's mom said before taking the spot beside her. Zora sat down on her other side while Silas took the loveseat.

"Mom, why are you home?" Zora asked.

"I've been working from home this week," her mom replied. "I'm not sure yet, but I may be back in the office next week." She ran her hand down Christina's back. "But it's a good thing I'm here." Then she turned to Silas. "So, what happened?" she asked.

"They had a patient who'd been recovering well suddenly go into cardiac arrest," Silas said. "It turned out Christina was the one who pressed the code blue button. They checked his potassium levels and found an insane amount, which they suspected someone had injected into his bloodstream.

"Christina wasn't authorized to be in his cubicle, so it made her a suspect, even though she'd raised the alarm. They were insisting it's a common tactic by perpetrators. But since there's no CCTV in the SICU to confirm if she was helping or hurting the patient, no other definitive evidence of her involvement, and Christina has no priors, they had no choice but to release her. Though they plan to keep her on the suspect list till further notice."

Zora turned to Christina. "What were you doing in his cubicle? I know he's not your patient."

"I got a text from you asking me to come there. You even gave me the cubicle number."

"Me? I never sent you a text."

"That's not possible." Christina placed the mug

she'd been holding on the coffee table and pulled out her phone. She scrolled through until she found what she was looking for. "Here it is." She handed the phone to Zora.

Zora accepted the phone and looked at the screen, and sure enough, the text message was bearing her name.

She shook her head in disbelief. "How is this possible?" She placed Christina's phone on her lap, pulled out her own phone, and checked her text messages. "See?" she said to Christina. "There's nothing here from me to you, and my phone has been with me this whole time. I wasn't the one who sent it."

"Someone must have spoofed the caller ID to make it look like the text was from Zora when it wasn't," Silas said.

"I agree," Zora's mom said. "Someone must have wanted Christina in that cubicle at that specific time."

Zora's mind spun. Why would anyone do that except... "Someone wanted you to take the blame for Eric Sawyer's death."

"Why?" Zora's mom asked. "I mean, it's not like you or Zora are related to this patient."

"I'm so sorry, Christina," Zora said, running her hands through her hair. It had been her fault.

Zora's mom looked from Christina to Zora. "What is it? What are you guys not telling me?"

"I reported the patient's illness as suspicious, since another patient had died the same way a few days prior," Zora said. "The hospital got the cops involved."

"Zora! Not again!"

"Mom, I really tried to stay out of it. I did everything I could not to get involved, but this patient showed up at the ER while I was on call. I had to do the best for my patient."

"Is this the only incident so far?"

"Well…"

"There are more? Please don't tell me the burglary is related to this."

Zora said nothing. She couldn't lie to her mom.

"Zora, you can't go through this again," her mom said with a shake of her head. "This has got to stop."

"Mom, I'd love for that to happen too, but the person behind this seems to be convinced I'm involved when I'm not. They won't give up. The only way out is to solve this case."

"Zora, this is too much. I can't lose you or Christina after what happened to your sister and Marcus. I won't let it happen. Please just stay out of it, okay?" Then she turned to Christina. "I think you need a shower and some sleep. Come on, let me take you upstairs."

Christina allowed Zora's mom to lead her up the stairs, and Zora watched them go.

Her mom was right. She shouldn't be involved.

But Zora sensed it was already too late.

23

"Silas, can I speak to you for a moment?" Zora said as soon as her mom stepped out of view.

"Sure. What's up?"

"Any updates on my sister's search? Were you able to find anything on that inmate?"

Zora hoped there would be some news. Any good news, no matter how insignificant, was welcome at this point and would take her mind away from her thrashed apartment and what had happened to Christina.

Silas leaned forward. "It wasn't easy, but we found a friend of hers who ran a racket with her for many years on the outskirts of Lexinbridge. It took some coaxing and five hundred dollars, but the woman mentioned that the inmate had a foster son and gave us his name. We're trying to track him down, but it's possible that he might have moved out-of-state after the inmate's death."

Zora's heart fell. It was both good news and bad news. Still, it was one step forward in the right direction.

"But don't worry," Silas said. "I'm more hopeful we'll find him since the woman said that he was a good boy that tried to stay out of trouble. But don't tell your mom yet. I'm waiting for more definitive news before I get her hopes up."

"What are you two talking about?" Zora's mom said as she came down the stairs.

No way was Zora spilling the news. "I thought you were helping Christina."

"I need to get her a jug of water and a glass in case she gets thirsty later."

Zora got up. "Why don't I help grab it and bring it up for you?"

"Would you? Thank you." Zora's mom turned and headed back up the stairs.

Zora's shoulders relaxed. Crisis averted.

But she hoped the next piece of news would be the big break they were waiting for.

24

Alisa entered the foyer of their home. She was tired after spending another day putting out fires at all their different businesses. She'd poured herself into the work, but it was still not enough to drown out the things that Pete had told her about Stewart.

On one hand, he was family and part of who she was, and on the other hand, the rumors inferred he was a sadistic murderer, something she recoiled from and wanted no part of. How could she reconcile the two?

Alisa shook her head to drive the thought away. Just dwelling on it was giving her a headache.

She reached her father's office. She was used to stopping by once she was back from work and saying hi. But somehow she couldn't bring herself to enter, even though the door was open. If the rumors about Stewart were true, then her father must have known about Stewart's activities and yet had condoned them. What did that say about him? Considering how she was feeling, Alisa feared her emotions might show once she faced her father. It was better to avoid it all together.

She turned to head toward her room, but the sound of Yegor's voice stopped her.

"I just confirmed that the woman at the cemetery was that lawyer that made the big splash on the local news many years ago," he said.

Cemetery? Alisa had been there recently.

"Why didn't you tell me this earlier?" her father said harshly.

"I'm sorry, boss."

"Do you think she saw her there?"

Saw who? Were they talking about her? Alisa leaned in closer to listen.

"I put someone on the lawyer who overheard some conversation about CCTV at the cemetery," Yegor said.

Her father banged his hand on his desk, and Alisa jumped and squeaked. She slammed her hand over her mouth, hoping they hadn't heard her.

But her father continued speaking, oblivious to what was happening outside his door. "So Alisa's mother might be looking for her."

Alisa froze. Her mother? Wasn't she supposed to be dead?

Her heart thudded. If her mother wasn't dead, then what had happened to her? Had her mother really been her father's loved one? Why wasn't she in Alisa's life? Had everything she'd been told over the years been a lie?

The questions crowded in, assaulting her, till Alisa found it hard to breathe.

She staggered, spun, and fled from the house.

Alisa drove aimlessly around the streets. Her mom was not dead. Then why had her father lied to her? Why? Who was she? By the time she realized where she was, she'd driven into the parking lot right outside Lexinbridge Regional Hospital.

Why had she come here? Sure, she'd been here a few times in the past to see Stewart. Was she yearning to see him? But Stewart was dead, and he wasn't the type to have listened to her sob story.

Instead, he would have made a mockery of it or used it against her.

Alisa let out a long sigh. She had nowhere else to go. Pete had gone out of town for the weekend for a rare visit with his friends, and she hated to disturb him. He'd come flying back, and that was the last thing she wanted. Maybe she should check into a hotel for a few hours before going home. She couldn't spend the night out, or her father would send his men to look for her.

Alisa made to leave, and that was when she saw her.

Dr. Zora Smyth had just exited the hospital doors and was walking down the side of the building, dressed in a medical coat over scrubs. This was the first time Alisa had set eyes on her, but she looked just like she had in the photo. What a coincidence seeing her right now, just when Alisa needed someone to talk to. Should she walk up to her and introduce herself?

Alisa shook her head. That was just ridiculous. And what would she say? *Hi, I'm Alisa, sister to Thomas Stewart, who ran the organ trafficking business and put you in detention.* Maybe she should just leave and check into a hotel in the area.

Then she noticed a guy in a black hoodie

following Zora. Alisa wouldn't have thought that was the case except the guy halted too when Zora stopped to pull her phone from her jacket, and started walking when she did the same.

Alarm bells went off in Alisa's head as Zora turned the corner and went out of view. She felt something bad was about to happen. Without thinking, Alisa jumped out of her car and raced toward where she'd last seen Zora. As the daughter of a crime family, Alisa had had her share of workouts and martial arts training so she could defend herself.

Alisa soon reached the corner and saw Zora still walking ahead, oblivious to the suspicious man following her. Then Alisa noticed a dark alley ahead. *That must be where he plans to attack her*, Alisa thought.

She removed her heels and ran with silent footsteps after them. She was just a few meters away when Zora made to cross the dark alley and the guy lunged at her.

Zora jumped back in surprise and then fought to free herself with a ferocity Alisa hadn't expected as the guy grabbed her arm and started pulling her further into the alley. Zora clawed at his hand and punched and kicked any part of his body she could reach. This slowed her attacker, but he didn't give up and continued dragging her.

Alisa soon reached them and noticed a metal rod lying in a corner of the alley. She picked it up and banged it on the head of the assailant.

The guy groaned and staggered, but Alisa didn't stop hitting him. Arms, back, shoulders, nothing escaped her rod. The assailant fell but didn't stay down for long, and as soon as he had scrambled to his feet, he ran away. Alisa attempted to go after him, but a hand held her back.

"Don't," Zora's calm voice said. "It's no use."

Alisa looked at Zora. She was more beautiful up close than the picture had conveyed with her wavy dark hair, stunning figure, and a genteel air. She could see why Stewart might have been enamored with her. But something about her seemed familiar, though Alisa couldn't put her finger on what it was.

Zora let her hand fall, and she gave Alisa a warm smile that lit up her face. "Thank you for helping me," she said.

Her smile warmed something inside Alisa and eased the ache in her heart. She couldn't help smiling back. "You're welcome."

Zora stretched out her hand. "I don't think we've met. I'm Dr. Zora Smyth."

Alisa accepted the proffered handshake. Zora's hand was soft and warm, just like she'd expected. "I don't believe we have. I'm Alisa Petrykin."

"Nice to meet you," Zora said.

"Me too." Alisa looked around. "Aren't you going to report the attack?"

Zora shook her head. "No." She chuckled. "I'm not exactly a fan of the cops."

Alisa laughed. "Me either."

Zora gave a quizzical look that wasn't uncomfortable. Though Alisa wanted to chat more with Zora, it wouldn't have been best considering the history between her and Stewart.

She let go of Zora's hand. "I have to go," Alisa said, and turned to leave.

"Could I buy you coffee tomorrow?" Zora asked from behind her. Alisa turned back to face Zora. "To say thank you, I mean."

Alisa stared at Zora's hopeful face. As much as she knew it wasn't right, she wanted to. It would also be a great way to observe Zora up close. "Sure," Alisa replied.

Zora's face broke into a smile. "Awesome. How about eleven a.m. at the coffee shop across the street?" Zora pointed to a shop with cute blue-and-white-striped awnings.

"That works," Alisa said. Then she cocked her head. "Did you hear something?" she asked.

Zora shook her head. "No. What's wrong?"

"Probably nothing. It must have been my imagination."

"Okay. It was nice meeting you, Alisa."

"Same here."

Zora gave her a small wave and walked off.

Alisa watched her go. *It's only coffee*, she thought.

What harm could it possibly do?

25

Zora didn't know what had made her ask Alisa out yesterday, but there was something about her that drew her in. All she knew was she was excited about meeting her again.

She'd spent another night at the hospital since her home was still a mess, and by the time ten-forty-five a.m. rolled around on Saturday morning, Zora was antsy to get going as she closed the medical magazine on the latest surgical technologies she'd found in the residents' lounge. Even Brian, who was on-call today and had stopped to see Zora, noticed.

"Are you going on a date?" Brian asked.

"Nope," Zora replied. "Why do you ask?"

"Because you look pleased as a punch."

"I'm just going to meet a friend."

"A friend, sure." Zora cuffed him playfully on his head. "Ouch! That hurts."

"Really?" Zora stared him down till Brian grinned at her. She chuckled as she shook her head. "It's not what you think. I just met someone who I think might just make a good friend."

"You can never have enough good friends," Brian said. "Either way, have fun. It's good to see you excited about something again."

"Thanks, I will," Zora said as she headed out.

Zora arrived at the coffee shop at five minutes to eleven and sat down. *Phew!* She'd made it on time. She looked around the place, but Alisa wasn't there yet.

That's fine, Zora thought as she sat down. It was better she'd arrived first.

A waiter approached her. "Would you like anything?" the young man with the mohawk asked.

"Can I have a glass of orange juice?" Zora asked. She loved her coffee, but somehow she felt orange juice was a better option for today.

"Coming right up," the young man said as he

beamed at her. He left and returned a few minutes later with the juice. "Here you go," he said.

"Thank you," Zora responded.

"You're welcome. Let me know if you need anything else."

Zora sipped her drink and waited for Alisa to arrive. She'd thought she'd be here by now, but maybe she was running late.

Twenty minutes later, Alisa had still not arrived.

Zora frowned. Was she no longer coming? The mistake she'd made last night was forgetting to exchange phone numbers with her.

An hour later, Zora was convinced Alisa was never coming.

Her shoulders slumped. She'd been excited for nothing. Maybe she'd been the only one eager for them to meet.

And maybe it had been her imagination that Alisa was interested as well.

26

Alisa closed the file she'd been working on. There, all done. She'd known that if she didn't take care of it, she wouldn't be able to focus and enjoy her time with Zora.

Only the thought of their appointment had helped her get through the night, sit through breakfast, and pretend she'd heard nothing. It'd taken an enormous effort not to blurt out the question: *who's my real mother?* She'd thought about it throughout the night, but was no closer to coming up with a plan.

Alisa checked her phone—it was time to leave. She donned her jacket, picked up her handbag, and headed to the door.

The door opened, and her father walked in, followed by Yegor.

Alisa's eyes widened. What was he doing here? Today was a Saturday, and her father had never come to the office on the weekend since she'd started working here.

"Alisa," her father said. "Where are you going?"

Unease snaked down Alisa's back. Why was he asking? Then Alisa realized her father had not called her by his endearment for her. "I have an appointment," she said.

"With who?" her father said in a mild tone. But Alisa knew better—she'd heard her father use that tone countless times and yet hurt the men he'd spoken to that way in the next minute. Something was wrong. By now, her father had moved over to the couch in her office and sat down. Yegor stood close to the doorway.

"With a friend," Alisa answered.

Her father glared at her. "Since when is Zora Smyth a friend?"

Alisa's eyes narrowed. "Have you been spying on me?"

"How could you meet someone who had a role in your brother's death?"

"Is that it, or is there something else?"

Her father's gaze did not falter. "You're not meeting with her. I forbid you to see her again."

"You can't stop me," Alisa said. "I can do whatever I like." She headed toward the door.

"Yegor, take the princess home and keep her there," her father said simply. "She won't be coming back to the office for a while."

"What?" Alisa said as Yegor grabbed her hand in a steely grip. "Let me go." But he instead dragged Alisa to the door.

"I said let me go!" she cried, and clawed at his grip. Alisa had seen Yegor handle men much bigger than him, but that didn't stop her from trying to free herself. Yegor merely grunted and dragged her through the door and down the hallway to the elevators.

But Alisa didn't make it easy for him. She was kicking and jabbing all the way. Unfortunately, Yegor was like a tree that refused to budge. He wasn't her father's right-hand man for nothing.

Then someone pressed a piece of cloth over her nose, and Alisa felt herself falling. Her arms and legs were weakening, but she couldn't stop it.

Alisa's world went black.

———

"Alisa, wake up." Someone was shaking her. Alisa opened her eyes to see Pete in front of her.

"Thank goodness you're awake," he said.

Alisa forced herself to sit up and looked around. She was in her own bed, still in the blouse and pair of jeans she'd worn to the office. But what was Pete doing in her bedroom? And where was Sparky?

"I've been so worried about you," Pete said as he sat beside her on the bed. "I thought you'd never wake."

"Pete, what are you doing here? How did you get in? Have you seen Sparky?"

Pete chuckled. "Hold on with the twenty questions. I'll answer the last first. Sparky is with your father and is following him around."

Alisa's shoulders relaxed. Sparky was in good hands—her father had always had a soft spot for him.

"I called your number a few times and guessed something was wrong when I couldn't get through," Pete continued. "So I took the next flight available and went straight to the office, figuring you might be there as usual. I found the place empty save for the cleaning lady, who whispered to me what had happened.

"I came over and your father granted me five minutes to see you and sent Yegor to open the door for me. Did you know your father changed the lock on your door so he could override your inside lock with a key he keeps on his person? No one else can enter your room without the key. What's going on?"

Alisa recalled all that had transpired since her father came to her office, and the tension in her shoulders returned. How could a man who called himself her father do this to her? His men had even made her pass out. How could her own father humiliate her like that? Maybe because she wasn't his real daughter.

Her shoulders straightened. She had to find out who she was.

Alisa got up and padded to her home office. Pete followed her. "What are you doing?" he asked.

Alisa turned and put a finger on her lips and then pointed upwards. Pete nodded.

She picked up a small remote from her desk and pressed play. Loud country music filled the air from the surround system. Then Alisa pulled Pete close enough to smell his aftershave.

"Pete, I need you to run a DNA test for me," she whispered into his ear.

"What?"

"Shh. Just listen," Alisa said. "I need you to run it

against a missing persons registry, but my dad can't find out."

Pete thought for a moment. "I know someone who can do that."

"Okay. Follow me." Alisa went to the bathroom and pulled out the cotton swab pack she kept handy in her cosmetic kit. She still needed something to put the cotton swabs in.

Then she remembered the tiny empty tubes she'd bought when she'd imagined making her own fragrances in her spare time. She headed back into her walk-in closet and pulled two tubes from the basket she'd stored them in. Alisa returned to the bathroom, picked up one of the cotton swabs, and put it in her mouth.

"Hold on," Pete said. He grabbed her mini scissors from her cosmetic kit and snipped off the end of the swab she held. "I read somewhere that you need to do this for about four of them."

"Thanks," Alisa said. She accepted the scissors from Pete and then cut off the ends from three additional swabs.

Alisa scraped the inside of her mouth with the first swab before inserting it into a tube and screwing the cover back on. She did the same for the remaining swabs, fitting in two swabs per tube. Then she handed the tubes to Pete. "Can you get them out without my father discovering them?" Alisa was pretty sure Yegor would search Pete on his way out.

"Don't worry, I know what to do," Pete said as he accepted the samples. He removed the insoles of his shoes to reveal a secret compartment.

Alisa's eyes widened. "Who would have thought? Why do you have these compartments in your shoes?" she asked.

"You don't want to know." He stashed a tube in each space, replaced the insoles, and put his shoes back on. "I'll remove them once I'm back at my place."

"Thanks, Pete. I don't know what I would have done without you."

Pete grinned at her. "Very little." Alisa cuffed the side of his head. "Ouch! You need to stop doing that."

"Thank you," Alisa said.

"But how do I reach you once I have the results? It seems your father confiscated your phone."

"Not a problem." Alisa walked over to her closet and dug out a box from the back. She opened it and pulled out a black burner phone.

"You have one of those?" Pete asked.

"I'm a crime boss' daughter, remember?" Alisa

called Pete's number with it. "Now you have the number," she said.

"Okay, I have to go. My five minutes must be up."

Alisa replaced the box back in its hiding place and flushed the cotton swab heads she'd cut off down the toilet.

"Go," she whispered to Pete as she climbed back under the bed covers. Pete left, and Alisa closed her eyes and pretended to sleep.

A few minutes later, her father came in and sat by her bed. Alisa kept her eyes shut. He brushed her stray hair away from her face and kissed her forehead. Then he stood up and left.

Alisa bunched her fingers into fists under the covers. She'd been a naïve young girl with no memories when her father had brought her home and showered her with affection. But now, she would dig into the truth about her past.

It was time to find out who she truly was.

27

Zora's phone rang as she headed into the hospital. She swiped the answer button. "Hello, Dave."

"Hey, Zora. How are you doing? I got back today and heard about what happened to Christina. Is she okay?"

"She's doing much better." She had stopped by to see Christina earlier—Zora's mom had been enjoying fussing over her. Zora brought Dave up to speed about the spoofed text.

"It fits," Dave said.

"What do you mean?"

"My colleague who examined your place thinks someone overrode your alarm system. It didn't even show up on your alarm company's radar, which is unusual given how good they are. It could mean someone skilled with computers did it."

"And with Christina having a spoofed text—"

"Exactly."

"So this is someone with advanced skills, a hacker likely."

"Right. I think this is an important clue if it's the same person behind the digoxin cases. It could shed more insight into how the perp is reaching the victims."

"Did they find who vandalized my apartment?"

"My colleague found a couple of fingerprints that don't match yours or Christina's."

"That would be easy to rule out. Christina and I don't invite folks over to our place. Even my mom hasn't been in it since we renovated it. We also know the small crew that handled the renovation, and none had a criminal history the last time we checked."

"Then, that's great. He's running the prints through the system. If we find one person, we might discover who else was involved—he's almost certain it wasn't a one-man job."

Hopefully, they would find the culprits. "Did your computer guy find anything about the numbers?"

"Not yet, but he hasn't given up. Orsville was also a dead end."

"I'm sorry."

"Don't be. It's not over till it's over."

"That's the spirit."

Dave chuckled. Then he said, "I'm confident we'll catch whoever is behind all this."

Zora believed the same.

She just hoped they would stop him before something worse happened.

ndy chuckled. From what he'd seen on the police report update, they'd found out about the alarm system override.

It wasn't a big deal. Even if the cops discovered more clues, they still wouldn't be able to trace it back to him. He was a ghost in the hacking world, who made sure his digital fingerprints didn't exist.

He thought about what he'd done to Zora's friend. It was all Zora's fault. Hopefully, she'd gotten the message to stay away from the case. He didn't want to harm them, but would if they stood in the way of his mission.

He bent down and rubbed the head of the stray cat he was feeding. Andy had spotted him rummaging through the garbage the few times he'd come by the apartment. But he'd seen the cat limping yesterday, so Andy had bandaged its leg. And today, he'd brought cat food to feed him. He was certain Sammy would have approved.

Andy continued rubbing the cat's head as he watched it eat. Sammy had liked cats and would always give them every scrap of food they had. It hadn't mattered to her if she'd stayed hungry instead. So much so he'd scolded her many times about it. But she'd always laughed his concerns away. Sammy would have loved this cat, and he could imagine her stopping by each day to nurse him back to health. She was like that, always helping those injured and helpless.

His heart squeezed in pain. Andy would give all the cat food in the world just to have her back. But she was gone forever, and that was why the man in the SICU had to die. He was the worst of his kind, pretending to everyone that he was this beloved family man, yet he was worse than the devil in secret. Andy would have loved to expose him for who he was. But it didn't matter now, since he was dead—he'd had to pay; they all had to.

He left the cat as it continued to eat. Unfortunately, Andy wouldn't be back here again—his mission was complete, and it was time to leave.

Eighteen down, two more to go.

29

Alisa sat up as her door creaked open. They'd locked her in her room for more than a day, and the only people she'd seen so far were the guards who brought her meals.

It could only be her father or maybe Pete, if her father had given him the key, since she'd engaged the lock. But Pete would have given her a heads up if he was coming. She assumed he'd stayed off the grid to work on the assignment she'd given him, though Alisa felt uneasy since she hadn't heard from him and couldn't reach him no matter how many times she'd called his number.

That left her father. Hopefully, he'd bring Sparky with him.

Her father walked into her room, followed by Yegor. "I'm glad you're awake," her father said.

No Sparky. Why? Alisa had missed him something fierce. She hid her disappointment and stayed quiet, watching her father. There had to be a reason he'd come, and she was sure she'd find out soon.

Her father took the seat closest to her bed. "He's not coming," he said.

Could her father be referring to Pete? *No way.* How would he have known she was expecting Pete, unless…? An uneasy feeling snaked down Alisa's back.

"Pete is being punished," her father continued.

Alisa's heart sank at his words. Had he caught Pete working on the assignment? How had that happened? No, she wouldn't speculate. She could only hope her father didn't know everything. "Why?"

Her father sighed. "He betrayed the code. Did you really think he could sneak out your DNA without my knowledge?"

Crap. He knew! Her father knew. *Hold on!* What was this about a code? "What code?"

"Our family code."

Alisa tensed and looked at her father in bewilderment. What was he talking about? "But Pete isn't a member of this family."

"He is."

Alisa's heart rate increased. "What's that supposed to mean?"

Her father rubbed his brow. "You shouldn't be so trusting. After all these years, you still can't tell Pete works for me?"

Alisa's breath caught, and her mind reeled at his words. Pete worked for her father? How was that possible?

"He's been working for us since law school. I needed you to stay safe, and he made sure you did nothing that put you in danger."

Safe? Anger swelled in Alisa's heart. Was that what he called it? It wasn't enough to learn that Pete, the man she'd thought of as her best friend, had betrayed her by working for her father all along. Now, she'd found out her father had been monitoring her as well. "You mean you were keeping tabs on me?" she asked quietly.

"I wanted nothing to happen to you. You, of all people, should know how much of a target I am. Getting to you is the easiest way to hurt me."

Alisa felt a sudden tightness in her chest, and her vision blurred. How could he? Tears burned behind her eyelids, but she forced them back. It didn't matter what his excuses were. Her father had broken her trust not only by monitoring her, but by choosing someone close to her to do it, the very person she'd shared so many private moments with over the years. In that moment, Alisa wondered if she'd ever known him.

But what if her father was lying about Pete being his lackey? She had to hear it from him. "I want to see him," she said.

"Why? I'm not sure that's a good idea," her father said. "How should I put it? He doesn't look too good."

"You beat him? Why? I thought he worked for you."

"He didn't report what you were up to!" her father said harshly.

Ah! So Pete must have had a pang of conscience, if everything her father had said about him was true. The more reason she had to see him. "Okay, but I need to hear from him how he betrayed me."

Her father studied her face for a moment. "Fair enough. Yegor will take you to see him. But I must warn you not to try anything funny."

Alisa gave a humorless laugh. "What could I possibly do at this point?"

Her father turned and nodded to Yegor, who led Alisa out of the room.

Alisa entered the basement with Yegor right behind her. She'd seen her father's men making their way into this place, but she'd never been in it. The large room had blackened windows, so no light filtered in or out. A few fluorescent bulbs lit up the open space. Then she noticed a man on his knees tied to one of the floor-to-ceiling beams.

"Pete!" she called out as she recognized him. Then she remembered he was supposed to have betrayed her, and her steps slowed as she made her way to where he knelt.

Pete lifted his head to look at her. His hair was matted with streaks of blood running down his face, one eye was swollen, his left arm lay useless at his side, and his hand seemed to miss a finger. His clothes were bloodied and ripped, like he'd been flogged. "You shouldn't be here," he said in a hoarse voice.

Her heart hurt just seeing him like this, but Alisa couldn't let her compassion overcome what she'd just heard about him. She had to know the truth. "Is it true?"

She watched him swallow and then grimace at the effort. Her father's men had done a number on him.

Her first instinct was to reach out and touch him, but she forced herself to hold back.

"What did you expect, Alisa?" he answered. "You were so easy to fool. You made my job easy."

Alisa slapped him. She recoiled at what she'd done, but he deserved it. "Your job? I thought you were my friend!"

Pete flinched in pain and then spat out some blood. "Friend? You should know by now that friendships are overrated."

Her heart tore at his words. "How could you?" she cried out.

Then Alisa noticed Pete had been running his right index finger over the surface of the floor. What was he doing?

"It was easy," he said. "The princess that needed to be coddled." But his finger kept making the same motion, like he was trying to draw something. Was he trying to pass a message to her?

Alisa yearned to look closer, but that would only bring attention to what he was doing. It was best to continue talking to him.

"Coddled?" she flung back at him. "So, when did you decide to side with my father? Before or after I saved you?"

"I'm grateful you saved me, but your father made

me an offer I couldn't refuse," Pete retorted. "I mean, who would turn down taking care of the fragile princess?" His finger kept making the same motion.

That was when it hit Alisa. He was drawing the cupid's arrow!

Alisa's mind scrambled to understand. Cupid's arrow? She could only remember discussing it one time with him in the years they'd known each other. It had been Valentine's day, and since Alisa didn't have a love interest that would send her flowers, she'd opted to plant some in the front garden. She'd taken a break under the shade of the large tree in the garden when Pete had stopped by. Why was he bringing it up? She had to continue with the charade to find out.

"I trusted you and told you everything," Alisa said to him. "How did it feel hearing all that and then going behind my back and reporting our conversations to my father?"

"Oh, it wasn't hard at all—it's not like it was actual labor, like cutting down trees. Once you've done it the first time and then the second time, it becomes easier. It's almost second nature now, since it's been a couple of years."

Cutting down trees? Then she remembered. *The tree!* She'd discovered a hidden cavity in the tree that looked great for hiding important stuff, and he'd joked about cutting the tree down and stealing all her treasure.

Suddenly, Alisa understood, and her heart quickened. She glanced at Pete, who gave a subtle nod even as the hurtful words continued to spew from his mouth.

So he'd left something there for her. It was time to end the conversation before Yegor caught on. "I never want to see you again," she lashed out even as she gave him an imperceptible nod and watched as he stilled his hand.

Then Alisa turned and walked out.

She couldn't help Pete now, but she could retrieve whatever he'd wanted her to have.

Alisa waited until the next morning. It wasn't easy staying still when all she wanted was whatever Pete had hidden for her. But patience was important here. If she'd gone right away, they would assume it was something he'd said to her, which would mean more monitoring for her and more punishment for him.

It felt strange not going to work like she'd done every week for the past few years. So Alisa didn't bother dressing up and just wore a blue T-shirt and jeans. When it was mid-morning, she figured it was time to visit the tree.

She unengaged the inner lock and knocked on her door from the inside.

The door unlocked and then creaked open. One of her father's men, Fredek, poked his head in. "What do you want, princess?" he asked. Fredek had been one of her bodyguards while in law school, and one of the few men in the family she knew very well.

"I'd like to take a walk in the garden and get some fresh air," she said.

Fredek shook his head. "I'm sorry, princess. Boss gave clear orders not to allow you leave this room."

Alisa thought fast. "Why don't you ask his permission? Tell him I need some sunshine and vitamin D for my skin. It's not like you guys won't still be watching me." Her father had always complained that she never got enough sunlight, so he might approve the walk for that reason alone.

"Okay." He shut the door and locked it back up. Alisa could hear his steps fade as he walked away. She didn't have to wait long before he returned. He unlocked the door and held it open for her. "You can come out, but it will only be for a few minutes."

Alisa stepped out and walked down the winding

stairs until she got to the main floor. Instead of taking the main entrance, she took the side French doors that led to the garden.

She inhaled a deep breath and exhaled. The air was much fresher; she hadn't realized how stifling it had been inside. She didn't head straight to the tree which sat in the middle of the garden, but wandered around examining the flowers and plucking a few. Then Alisa reached the tree.

"It's time to head back," Fredek said.

No! She couldn't allow him to take her inside just when she'd reached her destination. "Just a few more minutes."

Fredek shook his head. "I'm sorry, princess."

Her heart raced. She had to get the hidden item, no matter what. "Please, Fredek."

Alisa could see the shock written all over his face. She'd never begged her family's men for anything. It'd been natural that she got whatever she needed as the family's princess.

Fredek swallowed. "Okay," he said, "but only for a minute." He stood there and waited.

Alisa gave him an impatient look. "How am I supposed to enjoy the sunlight with you staring at me like that?" she asked.

Fredek grunted and stepped a few feet away to give her some privacy.

"Thank you," Alisa said. It would have to be enough.

She leaned against the tree at the spot where she assumed the cavity was and snaked her hand behind her back as she searched for it. Where was it? She was running out of time, and Fredek could insist she go in any moment now.

Sweat broke out on her forehead as her hand kept searching. Why wasn't it here? Had it all been for nothing?

Then Alisa saw Fredek headed her way.

Her heart thudded in her chest. Alisa wasn't the praying type, but she needed all the help she could get. *Please, God, help me,* she prayed.

Then her hand felt the cavity. She thrust her hand in, not caring if there was a dangerous insect taking shelter in that spot. Where was the item?

"It's time to go." Fredek had arrived where she stood and was reaching for her arm.

That was when her hand felt a small cylindrical tube.

Alisa grabbed it and stuffed it in the back of her jeans and hoped the bulge wouldn't be visible. "Okay," she said as she straightened.

Fredek dropped her back in her room, and Alisa's shoulders relaxed as soon as the door shut behind her. She locked it from the inside for good measure and maintained a calm exterior as she walked to the bathroom, shut the door behind her, and turned on the shower.

Alisa pulled out the cylindrical object and held it up. It had a cover, which she pulled off before tipping the object into her hand.

A tightly rolled sheet of paper fell out. Alisa dropped the cylindrical tube on the surface of the sink and then unrolled the sheet of paper.

It was the DNA result from the missing persons database.

Alisa's hands shook as she scanned the paper all the way through.

Then her eyes reached the section that listed possible matches, and she gasped.

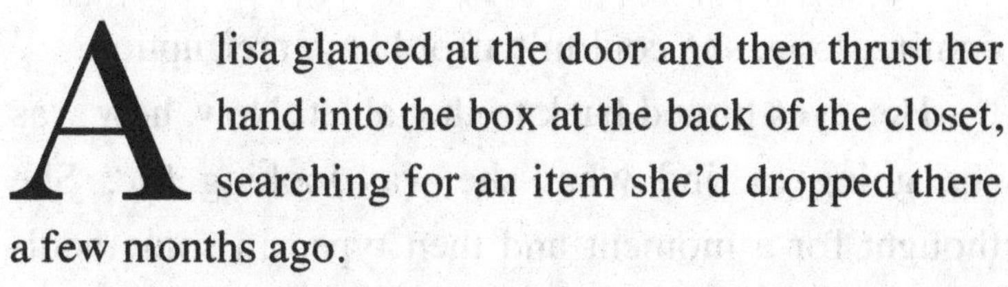

30

Alisa glanced at the door and then thrust her hand into the box at the back of the closet, searching for an item she'd dropped there a few months ago.

Her hand touched something smooth and cold, and she pulled it out. It was a tablet she'd stopped using when she'd upgraded her phone to the latest version that functioned both as a phone and a tablet. She searched the box again and then extracted a prepaid debit card she'd kept there as well.

She tucked both items under her shirt and headed into the bathroom, leaving the bathroom door ajar, which gave her a perfect view of her room's main door.

Alisa pressed the tablet's ON button, and it lit up.

Thank goodness it still had some battery charge in it, though it wasn't much. But it should be enough for what she planned to use it for. Alisa had never removed the sim card either, and she bought some data using the debit card.

She opened the search engine and typed in the name she'd seen on the report. A couple of search results came up. Then she narrowed it again by location, and one name appeared, but the information she was looking for wasn't there.

Alisa glanced at the door. She hoped no one was coming soon; she couldn't afford any interruption.

Her eyes turned back to the tablet. Now, how was she going to find what she was looking for? She thought for a moment and then typed in some additional search terms. She scrolled through a couple of pages and had almost given up when she found what she was looking for. *Bingo!*

Alisa stepped out, grabbed a pencil on her desk, and then returned to the bathroom. She wrote down the information she'd found on the reverse side of the report. Then Alisa folded the report until it was back to its former size and tucked it into her bra. No one would suspect she'd hidden anything there.

She turned off the tablet and replaced it and the debit card in their hiding place, and she was returning the pencil when she heard the rattle of the key in her door.

It had to be her father.

Alisa flew to her bed and dove under the covers.

The door opened, and Vaslav strode in.

Alisa's body went on high alert. What was Vaslav doing in her room? Her father was the only one who had the key, and there was no way he wasn't aware of the man's interest in her. Didn't he care any more about her if he'd allowed Vaslav to get close to where she was staying?

Her heart squeezed in pain. How could her father change so much in only a few days? But she didn't have the luxury to feel sorry for herself. Alisa had to stay alert. Fortunately, she'd trained in martial arts because of creeps like Vaslav.

"What do you want?" Alisa asked as her hand reached for the candle holder she'd started keeping under her second pillow after her father locked her in the room.

Vaslav looked around her suite. "So this is where the princess resides. I've been wanting to come in here for a long time."

"I said, what are you doing in my room?" Alisa said in a haughty tone, even as her hand curled around the stem of the candle holder.

He gave her a crooked smile, his teeth colored dark by the Russian cigars he liked to smoke. "No need to get all wound up. I just came to see how you're doing."

"Does my father know you're here?" The guy could very well have stolen the key or made a copy.

"It doesn't matter if he knows or not. He won't believe you after what you tried to do. Even the men outside," he pointed toward the door, "will deny it. And don't forget your brother is gone, so your father needs me."

Alisa gripped the candle holder so tightly it might have snapped. "Get out of my room," she said.

"Don't worry, I'm leaving." He spat out a glob of dark spit onto the floor.

Alisa almost retched. *Disgusting,* she thought. Vaslav was an animal, and she would rather die than have anything to do with him.

"I just came to see my precious property," he continued.

What did he mean? Was he hallucinating? Like that would ever happen. "I said, out!" Alisa insisted.

In the next minute, Vaslav was beside her, his

stinking breath fanning her face. She didn't know how he'd moved so fast. "I'll tolerate this insolence for now, but after you're mine, I'll punish severely for this," he growled.

Alisa glared at him. For someone like Vaslav, who thrived on fear, she would never show it, even though her heart raced and her stomach was all tied up. Her father had taught her that much.

He stared at her for a moment, his eyes raking over her body's silhouette.

Ugh! She would need a bath after this.

Then he turned and left the room.

Alisa's head collapsed back on her pillow as soon as the door shut. What just happened? Had her father abandoned her? No, she still had to believe that her father still cared for her somewhere deep down inside, even though he'd used Pete against her and kept her away from her mother. All his affection over the years couldn't have meant nothing, right?

But the danger she faced from Vaslav was real, irrespective of what was going on with her father. It was up to her to protect herself.

Alisa sighed. She had only one option left.

31

"Zora, we have a lead on the perp," Dave said in an excited tone.

Zora sprang to her feet and headed out of the residents' lounge. Luckily, the hallway was empty for a Monday morning, though not unexpected in this section of the hospital. Most of the traffic was in the clinics, the ER, and the OR. "What do you have?"

"We got some hits off the fingerprints in your room, and we brought the suspects in. Once they heard what they could be in for, they sang like birds for lesser charges. It turned out someone had put out a job on a site on the dark web and made it seem like it was only for a prank."

Zora leaned against the wall. "Dark web? What's that?"

"It's a section of the internet that fosters illegal activity. It's not indexed by search engines, so you have to be looking for it to find it. Most of the sites there are illegal to visit."

"So someone made my apartment a target there?"

"Yes, and paid these guys to do it. Unfortunately, it's hard to track down who ordered the job, but it sure fits our theory that the perp is a hacker."

"So he really is one." A thought occurred to Zora. "I just remembered something Mrs. Connelly mentioned to me in the ER. Her husband had had some symptoms that might have clued the doctors in on checking out his digoxin levels, and she thought she'd mentioned them to the ER doctor she'd first met. But the information was not in his patient notes. It struck me as weird at the time, but I'd forgotten about it. Is it possible the hacker deleted the information from the electronic medical records?"

"That could be, but we'd have to confirm with the ER doctor that they documented it in the first place."

"I can do that if you like," Zora said.

"No, I'll take care of it," Dave responded. "I believe I have the name of the doctor in my notes. I don't want you any more involved in this case than you are already."

"Okay, if you say so."

"Thanks for acquiescing to my request. I know it's a big deal, and I really appreciate the effort."

Zora chuckled. "You know me too well. You might find it easier getting the information than I can, since you'd be meeting him as part of the investigation approved by the hospital leadership. I, on the other hand, have no legal right to access his patient notes." She was no longer part of the medical reconciliation committee, so she couldn't even use that cover.

"True," Dave said. "I have one other piece of good news."

"What?"

"My computer analyst thinks he might have a bead on what the numbers are."

Zora's heart raced with excitement. "Really?"

"Yes, he found some online chatter about a similar set. He thinks it's a code that clients present to a certain hotel's concierge to gain access to special services."

That didn't seem like such a big deal. "Oh."

"I'm not done yet. From the amount of secrecy

involved, it could very well be some illegal services, like prostitution."

"But how would that be related to the digoxin cases? If the patients had been patronizing prostitution services, is that enough to get them killed?"

"Unless there was something else going on behind the scenes."

"In which case, Connelly and Sawyer could very well be perps."

"Exactly."

"So, let's say that was the case. Who gave us the note with the numbers? The killer or someone else?"

"Chances are higher that it's the latter. The killer is already taking care of them in his own way."

"So what's next?" Zora asked.

"I have a team going down to Orsville to work their contacts there and see if they can shake loose any information about which hotels are involved. I'll follow up with the ER doctor here."

"Good luck."

"Thanks, I'll need it. And Zora?"

"Yes?"

"Please stay out of trouble in the meantime."

Zora lifted her free hand in mock surrender. "Hey, I'm a peacemaker."

"Right."

Zora chuckled. "Why do I get the sense you don't believe me?"

"Of course I believe you. I'm your number one fan."

Zora's pager beeped, and she looked at the screen. It was the ER. "I have to go. There's a patient waiting for me."

"Alright, I'll talk to you later," Dave said.

"Thanks," Zora said, and then disconnected the call.

But Zora knew staying out of trouble was not up to her this time.

What if the killer attacked again?

32

A ndy ended the call as well.

His jaw twitched. Apparently, Dr. Smyth and her cop boyfriend had not stopped investigating the case. But one good thing had come out of it—they'd found out about the hotel code. Maybe it was time he helped their investigation along. He had nothing to lose by having the police shut those activities down.

"See why I told you we should bug her phone?" said his brother, who was also in the room and had heard Zora's conversation on speakerphone. "She's as persistent as they come from what I've heard about her." His brother had bugged her phone this morning when she'd left it in her locker and gone in for her first surgery case. "What are we going to do about her? We still have two more people on our list to take care of."

His brother was right. Dr. Smyth clearly needed a better lesson, one that would take up all her attention and force her to take her hands off the case. Andy ran his hands through his hair. "Give me a moment to think about it," he growled.

His brother uncrossed his legs. "While you're thinking about it, we won't use the usual method for the next bastard on our list."

Andy stared at him curiously. "Why?"

"There's no time. I'm going to handle him myself."

This was one of the few things he disliked about his brother. He could be very impatient.

"If we stick to our original plan, chances are we won't get caught," Andy insisted.

"I said I'll take care of it!"

Andy flinched. He hated when his brother was like this. There was no talking him down. It was better to just give in at this point. Besides, the result would be the same—death for number nineteen. "Okay, but no errors."

His brother stood and gave him a grin. "Have I ever made one? There were no issues when I took care of number sixteen at the hospital, right?"

Andy stayed silent. *That's because I always clean up your mess,* he thought, though he had to concede that number sixteen's death had been error-free. But Andy had been the one to plan out the death and then ensure that nothing showed up on the cameras. For number nineteen's case, he didn't know what his brother planned to do.

Hopefully, his brother wouldn't make any mistakes this time around.

33

The man hurried through the darkened streets. He'd overheard a rumor tonight, and he had to warn the others. Someone was picking them off one by one, and if his guess was right, he could soon become a target.

As much as he loved Orsville, this was not the time to stick around. Luckily, he had an older sister that had been asking him to visit her in Seattle. Maybe this was a good time to honor that invitation.

He cursed the day he'd met Eric Sawyer a year ago. Eric had been the one to convince him to join the club. Yes, he'd been interested, because who didn't like women? He'd heard the rumors and, like every other virile young man in town, hoped he'd one day get a chance to join the club. And his girlfriend had been pregnant at the time and no longer wanted sex. What was a man supposed to do?

Once Eric had given him the green light, he'd dressed in his best outfit and shown up at the Thirsty Bar—the club's primary location and meeting point. The club members, including leaders of Orsville and a councilman he'd recognized, had welcomed him heartily. It seemed Eric had paved the way for him.

After they'd had enough drinks, they'd moved the party to one of the ultra-private hotels in the area. The man had never been there before and had been overwhelmed by the opulence of the place. Once they'd ensconced him in a hidden lounge, he'd expected to see a few high-class call girls, considering the caliber of men in the club. Instead, they'd offered him a demur-looking girl for free to do with as he liked and to see whether he enjoyed a taste of the goods.

It had been heavenly. He'd thought matured women were the best at these things, but these high school girls could do things he never imagined. The man could feel the beginnings of an erection just thinking about it. He'd looked forward to his time with the girls every week, and his girlfriend seemed happy he was no longer pressuring her for sex. Who could beat that?

Then that stupid new teacher had appeared. She'd had the guts to show up at the Thirsty Bar to confront one of the club members. Hadn't anyone told her the place was off-limits to women? She'd spouted some nonsense about what horrible things they were doing, and how she was going to report it. He'd grimaced when he'd heard that. *Good luck with that*, he'd thought. Didn't she have any idea who she was dealing with?

They'd found her dead the next day. He hadn't expected them to deal with her in that manner, but it was her own fault for poking the hornet's nest. The police had questioned everyone. Nothing had come of it, since no one had seen or heard anything. All had returned to normal, and over time, some of their members had moved out to other towns and cities.

So, when folks had started dying off, he hadn't put two and two together. There'd been a drought in the town in recent times—a strange phenomenon for their part of the country—so the town's death rate had increased, and everyone just assumed it was because of it or some other sickness common at their age.

But tonight, he'd heard about what happened to Eric Sawyer and the ongoing investigation. Suddenly, everything had clicked into place. Someone was after them and killing them one by one. But who could it be? He couldn't remember if the teacher had any relatives, since her burial had been out of town. He could find out from his police contact if he wanted, but this was not the right time. It was more important to leave town and stay alive.

He felt a pang of conscience as he remembered his girlfriend and their young baby. It felt wrong leaving her behind, but didn't he have to be alive first to support her?

Besides, she could fend for herself. After all, she'd done well on her own all this time and had her mother. Yes, he'd send her a text telling her to move to her mother's. He'd wire money for her upkeep once he was in Seattle.

The man stumbled onto a large stone and went crashing down. Who'd left a stone here, for goodness' sake? This sidewalk, or even the road, wasn't under construction. He got up and dusted his pants. Then he noticed he'd ripped a knee.

He cursed under his breath, as he couldn't even go home and change. What if the killer knew where he lived? He would have to make do. So his plan was: get to the Thirsty Bar, inform the others, and head down to the train station. The bar was only the next street over, so he should be in and out and on his way soon.

But that was his last thought as a large object crashed against his head. His vision narrowed as he landed on the ground, and all he could see was a tall, dark figure holding a large object in both hands. The man tried to get up, but only managed to raise his head before he collapsed back on the ground. Blood dripped down the side of his head and into his eyes. He tried to lift his hand to wipe the blood away, but his arms felt so weak he couldn't move them.

Then something crashed into his head again, and his world darkened and then went out.

34

"Did you have to be so messy?" Andy scolded his brother. He'd heard about the death on the news.

His brother gave him a wicked smile. "Don't worry, I didn't leave any DNA behind."

Andy hoped so. The alternative was something he didn't want to think about. "Did you see the woman?" he asked.

His brother shook his head. "No, but she left a message, begging us to stop. She doesn't want any harm to come to *you*."

Andy felt a small regret that he'd involved her. He'd only accepted her help because she'd insisted. Now he wondered if it had been a mistake.

But he couldn't dwell on it now. Their revenge

was almost complete. Well, as long as no one interfered. To that end, he'd decided on what to do with Zora and had already put the plan in place.

He looked around the decrepit room. He was done here.

It was time to pack up and leave.

Nineteen down, one more to go.

Alisa waited all day, though she'd snuck her most important items into the bathroom and packed them in an emergency backpack she'd always kept around. But she couldn't delay any longer, since she wasn't sure what Vaslav was up to, and she had no plans to stick around and find out.

She wished she could take Sparky along, but Alisa wasn't sure how to locate where he was without risking exposure. As much as it pained her to leave him behind, she was sure her father would take good care of Sparky.

Alisa dressed in all black—T-shirt, jeans, jacket, and sneakers and pulled her hair into a ponytail. She turned off the lights, climbed into bed, pulled the covers over herself, and waited. As she'd expected, she heard the two guards leave her door after thirty minutes for a break. She waited an extra minute to be sure, got out of bed, grabbed and strapped on the backpack she'd hidden in the bathroom, and unlocked the door.

She opened the door as silently as she could and peeked out. No one was in the corridor, but she could hear their movements downstairs. She would have to make sure she stayed out of view till she left the area.

Alisa slipped out and shut the door behind her, sticking close to the wall as much as possible. She had to hurry, in case the men changed their minds. Alisa crept along the wall until she reached her destination—another room on the same floor.

She turned the knob. *Please, God, let it be unlocked,* she prayed. The door slid open, and Alisa slipped in and shut it behind her. Thank goodness no one had seen her.

Stewart's room still looked the same, and Alisa headed toward the alcove. All she needed to do now was find the entrance to his secret tunnel. She had to believe it still existed.

Alisa hastened to the alcove and began to touch and search the walls for a secret panel or button, but she found nothing.

Her heart rate quickened. Where was it? It had to be here somewhere. She searched the walls and then the desk and chair. Where could it be?

Then she heard a shout and the scurry of feet. Her heart rate galloped. They must have discovered she was gone. She had only a little time before they would think about searching Stewart's suite.

Alisa looked around the room. Where could it be? Had she heard wrong about it? Then she remembered she hadn't searched the floor. She got on her knees and pressed each marble square, but nothing moved.

Panic set in. She could hear the men searching each room, one after another, their footsteps drawing closer. They would be in Stewart's room soon enough. If they caught her now, her father would make sure they guarded her like Fort Knox. *God, please help me,* she prayed.

Then she noticed the light switch on the wall. She looked to check for the light fixture, but it had a shade with no actual holder for the bulb.

Bingo! She hurried to that section of the wall and pressed the switch. A panel on the floor behind the desk slid open. By now, she could hear the men right outside Stewart's door—there was no time left!

She hastened to the opening and spied some rungs on one side of the enclosure. Alisa lowered herself through the hole using the rungs, noticing a button on the wall next to them on her way down. She pressed it and watched the panel slide back in its original position just as the men burst into the room.

Alisa let out an exhale. They hadn't seen her. *Thank you, God.* Then she noticed she was still on a rung, and the passage was now pitch dark. Fear gripped her, but she refused to give into it. She could do this one step at a time.

She stepped down the remaining rungs until she reached the bottom. Then she was all clear. Alisa pulled out her burner phone and turned on its flashlight. The resulting illumination was a welcome change and gave her a chance to look around.

Alisa was in what looked like a tunnel. Cobwebs hung overhead from its ceiling, though the path appeared well-worn and dry. *Stewart must have used this a lot*, Alisa thought. The air felt cool and fresher than she'd expected.

Alisa shone the light in front of her as she made her way down the narrow tunnel. The occasional rat scurried by, and she tried her best not to jump, forcing herself to stay calm as she hurried along the tunnel.

The tunnel curved to the right and Alisa followed it. She could hear the occasional bark of a dog above her and even the incessant cry of a newborn, but Alisa didn't know where she was. After about fifteen minutes, and when she thought the tunnel would never end, Alisa happened upon a solid steel door.

This was it. Her exit to freedom. Alisa took a deep breath and turned the knob.

The door didn't open.

Crap! She was in trouble if she couldn't open this door. She could end up trapped in this tunnel or be forced to return to the house and face the wrath of her father, if she somehow got back in. Either option would ruin her, so she couldn't give up.

Alisa shone the flashlight on the walls around the door, searching for anything that stood out. Where could the secret button or switch that opened this door be? But she found nothing, no matter how much she checked.

Hope deflated out of her. She didn't know whether to cry or pull out her hair. She kicked the door in frustration, but her foot connected with the marble block on the floor beside it instead.

Ouch! That hurt. But then the door swung open.

Alisa's heart leaped, and tears rushed to her eyes. She'd done it! So the marble block had been the key. Who would have thought?

Then she noticed the door swinging right back.

What was happening? Well, she wouldn't stand here and find out. There was no time to waste.

Alisa hurried through the doorway and made it just in time as the door closed with a *thump* behind her. She adjusted the straps of her backpack, turned, and looked around in horror at the spacious white chamber she'd entered.

An operating table stood in the center of the room with what looked like a large steel trolley next to it. Stainless steel bowls of various sizes rested on top of the trolley, while an IV stand stood at its side. Rows and rows of instruments, some she recognized and others she'd never seen before, either hung on hooks or rested on shelves on the walls. The low humming of a ventilation system whirred in the background, but still it was not enough to remove the stench of stale roasted flesh that hung in the air.

Alisa shuddered. Even though everything looked pristine, she could tell this was a place of horror. Why was all this equipment here, and why was the chamber connected to Stewart's room?

Then she realized what this place was, and she gasped. This was Stewart's office that Pete had talked about!

The enormity of what Stewart had been hit her like a punch in the gut.

Alisa staggered as bile rose in the back of her throat. How could he have done such terrible things? Why? It was as if she could hear the voices of the victims crying out to her from the blood that had been spilled here.

She had to leave. She wanted nothing to do with this place that deserved to burn to the ground.

"Alisa."

Alisa gasped and turned. Fear gripped her.

She'd recognize that voice anywhere.

36

Adrianna Smyth exited the grocery store, humming to herself as she pushed the cart in front of her. She'd decided last minute to prepare a special dish for Christina, and even though it was late at night, she'd made a quick stop at the twenty-four-hour grocery store to pick up some food. Adrianna did some shopping now and then, but it had been a while since she cooked for anyone, and she was looking forward to it.

She soon reached her car and popped the trunk open. Adrianna transferred the bags and then stared at the filled trunk—she'd bought more than she needed. It was all good. She'd let none of it go to waste, even if it meant forcing Silas to try dishes he'd never heard of.

She smiled at the thought of him. Silas, the partner and friend who'd stood by her side all these years. It had taken her a long time to get over the loss of her beloved husband, but she was ready for a fresh breeze of love and friendship in her life. How he'd stayed by her side without putting pressure on her had been a miracle, and she cherished every moment of their developing love.

And now her joy was going to be complete. It was possible she was going to meet her long-lost younger daughter again! She could feel it in her bones just as sure as she was that blood was flowing through her veins. Adrianna knew Silas was hiding some information from her, but she'd worked with him long enough to know he would tell her when it was right. That was how much trust they had between them. She was sure it wouldn't take long.

Adrianna had no illusions about how her daughter would be, and it didn't matter—she would love her hard just the same. Of course, everything wouldn't be perfect, but Adrianna preferred it this way, since it would motivate her to remain thankful that she'd reunited with her in this life.

She closed the trunk and got in the driver's seat. It would only take her about fifteen minutes to get home. Christina would be awake by now, waiting for her. Adrianna had left a note for her on her nightstand.

She turned on the ignition and left the parking lot. Soon the road exited onto the freeway, and she accelerated. The traffic had eased for the day and she was thankful for that, otherwise the fifteen-minute trip would have turned to an hour. She hummed a tune to herself as she headed down the highway, mindful that her exit was coming up soon.

She slowed down a bit, turned on the signal, and entered the right lane.

Her phone's ringtone echoed in the car. Adrianna inserted the wireless Bluetooth earpiece into her ear. "Hello, Silas," she said.

"Hey, Adrianna, where are you?"

"I'm on the freeway, but I should be home soon." She pressed the brake to slow down some more. "I'm just about to turn off."

"Do you want me to call you back?"

"Up to you. I have the earpiece in my ear."

Her exit was coming up. Adrianna pressed the brake to slow down again, but this time the brake didn't respond.

"What's going on?" she muttered.

"What is it?"

Adrianna pressed the brake again. No response.

"Adrianna, is everything alright? Talk to me."

Fear wrapped its icy hands around Adrianna's heart, and cold sweat broke out on her forehead. This shouldn't be happening. She'd had her car serviced last week, and it'd had no brake problems.

But she had to stay calm. Adrianna would be alright as long as she didn't panic. She had a daughter who needed her, and another she was supposed to meet. She could do this. Adrianna turned on her hazard lights. "The car's brakes are not working," she said in a calm tone that belied her anxiety.

"What?" She could hear the alarm in Silas's voice. "Where are you?"

It was time to focus. She could make the exit without hurting anyone. *Thank you, God, that the freeway is relatively empty*, she thought. It could have been worse. "I'm going to make the turn now. Hang on."

Adrianna kept her eyes peeled between the road in front of her and the rearview mirror and then got on the exit that led to one of Lexinbridge's main streets. Fortunately, the nearest car ahead of her was so far away that her speed didn't matter. *Thank you, God*. But she knew it could change any moment.

"Are you okay?" Silas said over the line.

"I'm fine. I made it, but I need to find a side street

ASAP."

"There should be one ahead called Grange Street. It should be right before the first traffic light and is quiet at night since it's more commercial. You can do this."

Adrianna searched the street signs as she drove past. Grange Street, Grange Street... Where was it?

Her pulse ratcheted up. She could see the traffic lights in the far distance, and there was no Grange Street yet. Adrianna's palms became sweaty on the steering wheel.

What was she going to do if she didn't find the street? *No, stay calm, Adrianna. Keep looking.*

Her eyes scanned the streets that flew by. *Where are you, Grange Street?* By now, the cars ahead of her were slowing and drawing closer. *Oh, God, help me!*

Then Adrianna spotted the sign ahead and let out a sigh of relief. "Found it," she said. *Thank you, God.*

"Great," Silas replied. "I'm already in my car and on my way to you. I should meet you there shortly."

More cars had entered the main street by now, and it was time to get off it before she caused an accident.

Adrianna swerved into the narrow Grange street, bouncing off the edge of the curb. She fought to keep the car under control and finally straightened it out. The bump had slowed the car somewhat, but it still wasn't enough.

Then Adrianna spotted a car headed her way. At her speed, she wouldn't be able to stop to let the car pass. She honked at the oncoming car, but it didn't slow down or stop.

"Adrianna, talk to me," Silas said in a calm voice.

By now, her heart was pounding. "I'm on the street, but there's a car coming toward me that's not slowing down." The danger wasn't over yet.

Right then, Adrianna spotted a parking space in front of a commercial building coming up on the right. There was a large dumpster in front of the free spot. Maybe it would be enough to bring her momentum to a stop. "I think I know what to do," she said.

Here goes. She swerved the car to the right to get into the spot and managed to avoid the oncoming vehicle.

But her car spun instead. The crunching sound of crushed metal filled the air as she hit the dumpster and then crashed into a parked car before coming to a halt behind it. Her airbags exploded toward her.

"Adrianna! Are you okay?" Silas said. "Talk to me!"

37

Alisa stared at her father standing in front of her. He looked different, older and tired, the opposite of what she'd expected. Yegor was nowhere in sight.

"I knew you would come here," her father said.

"How?" Her eyes flitted around to identify the room's exit. Yes, there it was.

"I knew you overheard Stewart and me that day. I planned it that way."

That caught her attention. "Why? You could have told me directly."

"And have Stewart throw a fit? He would have destroyed the tunnel just to make sure you never got a chance to use it."

So he'd known Stewart's true nature. She had to ask. "Why didn't you stop him?"

Her father swept his hands around the room. "You mean this? He's my son, and he was what he was. He would have made a good leader for the family."

No, he wouldn't have, she thought. He would have drowned it in blood, the very thing the family was moving away from. Or was it? "Why did you have me work on the legitimate businesses?"

"Because I believe the family needs it for its future."

"But would you ever move away from violence if it were possible?"

Alisa's father looked at her like she had two horns. "It's part of who we are. If we let down our guards, another group will strike us, even from within."

Alisa's heart twisted in pain. No, she had to believe otherwise. She refused to accept everything she'd done, including the long nights and endless work weekends, had been in vain. She'd given them options if they ever decided to leave the bloody road they travelled. Alisa hoped they would.

But what her father had said reaffirmed what she'd always known—the family's path was not for her. She didn't know what awaited her in the future, but it would be better than this. She'd done her best for the family and could leave with a clear conscience, except for one thing. "I'd like one favor," she said.

"What?"

"Let Pete go. I mean, free from the family."

He cocked an eyebrow. "You still like him, despite knowing the truth about what he did?"

Pete had hurt her, but he'd helped her too over the years. "He's my friend."

Her father stayed silent and then nodded.

Alisa's shoulders relaxed. Her father always kept his word. Now if only he didn't stand in her way. "Are you here to stop me?" she asked.

He stared at her for a few moments. Alisa wondered what was going through his mind. As much as she didn't want to admit it, she was going to miss him. Despite everything. He'd been a good father to her, irrespective of what the family represented. Then he pulled out a dog carrier from behind him and held it out to her.

Alisa's heart leaped. Sparky! But wait! Was her father helping her? She looked at him in confusion.

Her father sighed. "Go. Don't ever come back here."

"Wait—"

"I said go! Take him and go. I never want to see you again."

His words were like slaps to her face, and Alisa stumbled. She grabbed the doggy carrier, turned, and ran toward the exit, only stopping once to look back. Her last look at the man who'd loved her and raised her as his own.

Her father stood there silent as a sentry.

Then she faced forward and ran toward her freedom.

natoly Petrykin watched Alisa leave and forced himself to stay where he was instead of running after her. His harsh words had hurt her, and while it had pained him to do so, it was the only way to stop her from ever coming back and allow her to live the carefree life she deserved. He'd placed her on house arrest and pretended not to care about her, so that she could leave worry-free. The family was no place for someone like her.

She deserved so much more than he'd ever given her. He'd wronged Alisa by keeping her from her family, but she'd been the best thing that ever happened to him. She'd softened his heart, and now he found it hard to go back to the hardened mobster he'd been.

He had no family left, and Anatoly's heart felt hollow at that thought. But it made what he was about to do easier. He'd found out Vaslav had approached Alisa, the one thing he'd warned members of the family never to do, and he couldn't wait to put the bullet between his eyes, not to mention those of the guards who'd ignored his order.

He turned and walked back toward the tunnel.

It was time to put the family back under his tight leadership like it was supposed to be.

Zora saw the missed calls from Silas as she picked up her phone from her locker. What could be so urgent that Silas had called her multiple times while she was in the OR? Did he have any updates about the search for her sister?

She grabbed the nearest chair, sat down, and then dialed his number.

"Zora, where are you?" Silas asked.

"I just finished from the OR. I'm in the call room now." Zora leaned back in her chair. "What's up? I saw your missed calls."

"Your mom just had a car accident."

Zora's heart somersaulted as she sat up. "How is she? Is she okay?" *Please, God, let nothing happen to my mom, especially not now,* she prayed.

"She's fine," Silas said from the other end of the line.

Zora's shoulders relaxed. "What happened? I thought she was supposed to be at home."

"She wanted to prepare a special meal for Christina and took a trip to the grocery store. Her brakes failed on her way back, but she was able to turn into a quiet commercial street where she hit a parked car. Luckily, no one was in the other car. She's fine, just shaken by the entire ordeal."

"Where is she right now? I'm on my way." By now, Zora had gotten up and was pulling her regular clothes from the locker. This was a family emergency. She'd call her attending and then reach out to Brian to see if he could come in and take over the rest of her call.

"She says I should tell you not to bother. We've finished with cops and doctors at a nearby ER have seen her. We're now at the mechanic trying to figure out what happened to the car, and we will head home in a few minutes. Hold on." Silas stepped away from the line and then came back a few moments later. "This is more serious than we thought, Zora."

Zora stilled. "What is it?"

"The car appears fine, except its computer

systems were infected by malware. The mechanic suspects someone might have hacked into them."

Zora couldn't believe what she was hearing. "Are you saying someone tried to mess with my mom's car?"

"Yes, someone may have tried to harm her. Zora, your mom's calling me. I have to go. I'll talk to you later." The line went dead.

Zora ran her free hand through her hair. First, her apartment, then Christina's spoofed text, and now her mom's car system. Could it be the same person?

And why? She'd done little in the past few days about the case, except…

She looked at the phone in her hand. Could someone have hacked it too? Had the perp heard her last conversation with Dave?

She tossed the phone into her locker like it was a rattlesnake. It may not be bugged, but Zora couldn't take the risk. She'd buy a disposable phone and SIM card on her way home. Because, yes, she was going home to see her mom, contrary to what she'd requested.

Zora had to see for herself that her mom was fine.

But first she had to contact Brian and the attending.

"Mom, are you okay?" Zora asked as she rushed to where her mom sat on the brown couch in the living room.

Her mom gave her a warm but tired smile. "I'm fine." She patted the space beside her on the couch, and Zora plopped down. "I told you not to come."

Zora waved her concern away. "Don't worry, Brian is covering for me. How are you feeling?"

"I think I'll feel better after I've gotten some nice long sleep. I should be as good as new tomorrow."

"You got me scared."

"I'm sorry." Her mom pulled her into a warm embrace.

"I'm just glad you're okay. I heard what Silas said about the car."

"I know. I'm just relieved the attack was on me and not on you." Then her mom released her. "But Zora, I worry about you. Can we try to stay out of these kinds of cases?"

Zora made to protest, but her mom held her hand up. "Yes, sometimes the case lands on your lap and you can't help being involved. I know you tried hard to stay out of this one. But could you try a little more to abstain till the end?" Her mom brushed a stray tendril of hair away from Zora's face. "Just try a little harder, okay? I just want a peaceful life for you."

Zora gave her mom a small smile. "I promise."

Her mom relaxed back on the couch. "Thank you."

Zora looked around. "So where's Christina?"

Her mom chuckled. "Can you believe that girl is still sleeping? It must have been exhausting working with the cleaners to put your apartment back together again."

"I feel bad about letting her do all the work." Christina was still on leave and had offered to handle the clean-up of their apartment.

"Well, you could make it up to her in other ways. I'm sure she'd love a thoughtful home-cooked meal."

"Mom, are you really suggesting that, when you know what a horrible cook I am? Are you trying to get her poisoned?"

Her mom laughed out loud and then winced as she held her side.

"Sorry. Are you okay?" Zora said.

Her mom chuckled. "I'm fine. It's just a friction burn from the seatbelt."

"Ouch."

"It's okay. As I was saying, if you work on one simple dish, no matter how many times it takes you to get it right, and give it to her, I'm sure she'll appreciate it. Just don't do it in my kitchen. I have no plans to renovate it soon."

"Mom!"

"Zora, are you giving your mother a hard time?" Zora looked up to see Silas coming in from the kitchen with a plate of sandwiches, two glasses, and a jug of water.

"Mom, *your boyfriend* is implying that I leave you to rest."

"My boyfriend is good, isn't he?"

Zora's mouth hung open. "Silas, you've been owned."

"I enjoy being owned by your mother," Silas replied as he placed the tray on the coffee table. A smile teased the corners of his lips.

Zora shook her head. "You two are crazy."

Her mom's phone rang at that moment, and she picked it up. "This is Adrianna Smyth." She listened and then held out the phone to Zora. "It's for you. What happened to your phone?"

"I'll tell you later," Zora whispered as she accepted the phone. "This is Zora Smyth."

"Zora, it's me, Dave."

Zora got up and walked toward the kitchen.

"I tried your number a couple of times, but it just rang through," Dave said. "Are you okay?"

"Sorry, I left it in my locker." She explained her theory about the phone being bugged and told him about her mom's accident.

"I'm so sorry to hear about your mom. Is she okay?"

Zora walked into the kitchen and leaned against the large black granite island in the center of the room. "She's shaken up but ok."

"That's good to hear. You may be right about the phone bugging. It's better to be safe than sorry. It might even be good to change your phone number altogether."

"That's what I plan to do with this new SIM card I bought. Any updates on the case?"

"The ER resident confirmed he'd taken the history of the digoxin-like symptoms, but he had to leave the ER on a personal emergency before the attending reviewed the case. It seems the history he'd documented disappeared from the records within that time frame."

"So our hacker was at work," Zora stated. "The attending wouldn't have prescribed clarithromycin if he'd known about the symptoms. It probably made the digoxin toxicity worse."

"Thanks for putting that into perspective."

"You're welcome."

"I have better news for you," Dave said. "We've identified the hotels that provided those extra services. It turned out the 'special' services include access to high school girls drugged to 'keep them in a happy state' while they attended to the men. We found some of the girls in the basement."

Zora gasped. "Isn't that kidnapping and statutory rape?"

"Some of them are underaged, so clearly statutory rape. We're still figuring out the evidence for the rest. We heard from the girls how it worked. These men show an interest in the girls, force their parents to release them one way or the other, and then bring them to the party where they're drugged and used. The girls are allowed to go home the next day, and the cycle is repeated. Only a few remain at the hotel, and those are usually runaways who prefer to stay off the streets. So, it's going to be hard pinning kidnapping charges on these perps."

"But what about their families?"

"Some are from the area. They'd received threats and are too frightened to say anything. A few were paid off with hush money. It seems these perps target girls from low-income families. Some girls are also from nearby towns who ran away from home and ended up in Orsville. But none are from outside the state, otherwise the feds would have been called in."

"That's horrible."

"We caught some of the perps at the hotel, but a few escaped. But we're not giving up until we get them all. Bastards."

"I'm glad. They deserve to fry in hell for doing this to innocent girls."

"I agree," Dave said. "One girl even mentioned a Samantha Pratt, her high school teacher, who'd tried to stand up for her. The last she heard was that the teacher had been murdered."

Zora was stunned. It was terrifying to think that something like this had happened so close to her hometown.

"But here is where it gets interesting," Dave continued. "Another girl overheard the men talking about how some of the perps had been dying lately. They mentioned the names Sean and Eric. The men seemed worried and wondered if it had anything to do with the death of the schoolteacher. The girl had pretended she was still drugged and listened to everything they said."

"Brave girl. Could it be…?"

"I think so. Our hacker may be the one behind the

death of the perps, and if they had something to do with the schoolteacher's death, then vengeance for her murder might be the hacker's motive. If other perps have died, then he's killed more than the two victims we're aware of."

"I wonder how the hacker is related to the teacher," Zora said. "Did she have any relatives like a sibling or even a fiancé?"

"That's what we're trying to track down. Right now, the only thing we have is her picture from the school records. She must have liked cats because she's wearing a turquoise cat pendant in it."

Zora's heart rate quickened. "Wait a minute," she said. She'd seen a similar pendant somewhere, one with a little black smudge on it. *Think, Zora, think.* Then it came to her. "Could you send a copy of the picture to this phone? I think I've seen someone at the hospital with a similar necklace."

"Sure. Hold on."

Zora heard a ping on the phone. She opened the text to see the image of a strikingly beautiful brunette with a warm disposition about her. *She must have been a wonderful teacher,* Zora thought. Then she noticed the pendant on her neck and the cat had a smudge on its nose!

"Dave, I think it's the same pendant. It even has

the same black smudge! I saw a patient care assistant, Drew Francis, wearing the same necklace. He's assigned to my department's ICU, and the nurses even praised his care of Eric Sawyer!"

"We need to speak to him. I'm on my way to the hospital now. Thank you."

"I'm glad to be of help."

"I have to go."

"Talk to you later." Zora ended the call.

Unbelievable. She was glad Dave and his team had saved the girls. They would require lots of counseling after what they'd been through, but she hoped they'd fight through it for a chance at a better future. She'd checked with Dave later to see if there was any way she could help.

Now, what if Drew Francis was really related to the case? It'd been a miracle Zora had seen the pendant. Well, that was one puzzle Dave would have to figure out.

Zora straightened and then moved from the kitchen back into the living room.

Then she noticed her mom shaking like a leaf.

40

S ilas held her mom in his arms as Zora rushed to her side. "Mom, what is it? Are you okay?" She glanced at Silas, and his face was grim as well.

"We're on speakerphone," Silas said, pointing to his phone on the coffee table. "It's about your sister." Then he spoke in the phone's direction. "Helen, please go on. It's only Zora." Helen was one of her mom's employees, and she worked under Silas.

Zora's heart raced as she settled into the loveseat opposite her mom. *Please, God, let it be good news,* she prayed.

"Hello, Zora," Helen said warmly.

"Hi, Helen."

"As I was saying," Helen said in a more business-like tone, "we found the inmate's foster son working as a warehouse manager on the outskirts of the city. A mild-mannered young man. We had to wait until he was off duty before he could speak with us. It turned out the inmate kept a diary, which he'd preserved all these years. Who would have thought? Anyway, we followed him home, and he handed it over to us. It turned out the diary had some important information."

Zora's heart quickened, and she watched her mom take a deep breath and exhale. This was it. Maybe this was the clue that would change everything.

"The woman detailed how they'd kidnapped the wrong girl. By the way, the date on the entry matched the date Mrs. Smyth's daughter went missing," Helen continued. "When the client who'd given the order discovered what had happened, he wanted them to return the girl, but then the news of the missing girl broke on the media."

Zora gasped as her mom took a sharp inhale. At this rate, Zora hoped her mom wouldn't go into shock. Silas rubbed her back and held her close.

"What else?" Silas asked.

"They couldn't return her anymore, and the client adopted the girl. The inmate thought it was wacko, but she said nothing. It wasn't her business anymore after being paid. And besides, she wanted to stay alive."

"Did she mention the name of her client?" Zora asked.

"No," Helen responded. "But there was one more entry. The little girl's name was Alicia."

Zora's mom collapsed on Silas.

41

Zora rushed to her mom's side and shook her gently. "Mom, are you okay? Speak to me!"

Her mom opened her eyes. "I'm fine," she said in a tired voice. "It was just a little shocking."

"Oh, Mom!" Zora said.

"Good job, Helen," Silas said to the speakerphone. "You guys can take tomorrow off."

"Thank you, sir."

Silas disconnected the call. Then he turned to Zora's mom. "Do you need to lie down?"

Her mom shook her head. "I'm fine." Then she seemed to remember what Helen had said. "My poor baby," she said, as her voice cracked. "She must have been so frightened." Zora's mom broke down and sobbed. Silas gathered her into his arms and lent her his shoulder.

Zora had never seen her mom look as broken as she did. How she'd held herself together all these years without collapsing was a miracle.

"Your mom never forgot your sister, not even for a minute," Silas said. "She tracked down every rumor or clue and paid thousands of dollars to investigators to keep searching, no matter the state or country. She just wanted your sister back. That's why she worked so hard. To make enough money to keep funding the investigation and take care of you. And she blamed herself all the time. She felt she'd let you and your sister down."

Zora stared at her mom's back. She hadn't known. Until the past few years, she'd thought her mom never cared and was too engrossed in her work. But then she'd realized her mom loved her, and they'd been working through their differences ever since. Now she finally knew the truth.

Zora waited till her mom's sobs subsided. Silas handed her mom a glass of water, and she gulped some of it and nursed the rest. "So what now?" she asked.

"We're going to do our best to track down the inmate's boss," Silas said. "This sort of person works with different clients, so it might take a while. But we won't give up."

"Unless a miracle happens," Zora said.

The doorbell rang.

Zora looked at her mom and then at Silas. "Are you expecting anyone?"

Her mom shook her head as she wiped her tears. "No."

Zora got up. Who could it be? She made her way to the door's security camera and looked at the screen.

Her eyes widened. Zora pressed the door release button, and the steel door opened. "What are you doing here?" she said.

"Who is it?" her mom asked, coming up behind her.

Then Zora jerked at the sound of glass crashing to the floor.

"Why?" the man asked on his knees, his eyes wide open in horror at the gun pointed at his head.

"You shouldn't have killed her, Arnold. Samantha Pratt. Remember her?" the woman said. She'd known the twentieth victim would try to escape out of the town, and she'd tracked him down to his car.

"The schoolteacher?" Then the man's eyes narrowed. "What does it matter to you?" he snarled.

"She was like a daughter to me," the woman cried out. "That girl burrowed her way into my heart, even though she was just a tenant, and became the daughter I never had." She gripped the gun more tightly. "You stole her from me. Did you think you'd get away scot-free after killing her?"

"I'm sorry," the man said. The woman could see Arnold's pants turning wet at his crotch.

"It's too late," she said.

The woman pulled the trigger, and her hand jerked.

Arnold collapsed on the floor. His eyes stared blankly, and blood mixed with brain matter spilled from what remained of his head.

The woman tossed the gun next to where he lay in the parking lot and left.

It was over.

Time to surrender herself at the police station.

Twenty down, zero to go.

43

Zora turned to see her mom standing behind her, her face deathly white.

She glanced from her mom to Alisa and back. Why did her mom look like she'd just seen a ghost?

And then it clicked. The same honey-colored hair, the cheekbones… so that was why Alisa had looked somewhat familiar when they'd met earlier. Could it be…?

"Alicia," her mom murmured, taking a shaky step forward.

Zora's hand flew to her mouth. *Oh, my goodness gracious.*

"Hello, Zora," Alisa said. "Can I come in?" Alisa was dressed in all black and carried a backpack.

Zora was still shell-shocked, but she stepped aside. "Please come in."

Her eyes followed Alisa as she entered their home. Could it really be her sister, standing here in the family living room? Wasn't it only a few minutes ago they'd wondered when they'd find her? Now she was standing right in front of them. Miracle of all miracles!

Zora pinched herself. *Ouch!* It was not a dream. She stared at her sister. Alisa did look like her mom's younger replica. How had she missed this?

"Alicia!" Her mom ran forward and grabbed her into a hug. Alisa's arms hung awkwardly at her sides. It must have been a shocker for her too, meeting the family she didn't know she had. But how had she known to come here?

"Mom, let the girl breathe." Zora freed Alisa from her mom's embrace, but her mom clung to Alisa's hand like she'd never let go. Zora led them both to the couch.

Silas stood up as they approached and moved over to the second loveseat. He gave Alisa a warm smile. "I'm Silas Park, a friend of the family."

"Nice to meet you, Silas," Alisa said.

"Sit," Zora said. Alisa and her mom sat next to each other. Zora took the loveseat she'd been on. "So,

Alisa, I still can't believe you're here. How did you know—"

"You were my sister?"

Zora nodded.

Alisa sighed. "It's a long story. I found out a few days ago my mother was still alive. I've always been told she was dead, so imagine my shock." She pulled out a sheet of paper from the pocket of her jacket and handed it to Zora.

Zora opened the document. It was a report from the missing persons database in Texas, and it matched Alisa with Zora and her mom. Zora and her mom had added their DNA to the registry many years ago. She passed the document over to Silas. Zora was certain he'd confirm the authenticity of that document. "But what about the day we met?"

Her mom's eyes turned sharply to Zora, "You've met before?"

"She saved me from an attacker a couple of days ago."

"An attack? Why am I just hearing about this?"

"Mom, that's not so important now," Zora said gently. Then she turned to Alisa. "Was it a coincidence?"

"It was totally random. That was the day I found out my mom was alive. I was driving around in shock when I ended up in the parking lot of the hospital. I recognized you from the news when I saw you come out. But then I noticed the strange man following you. I sensed he was up to no good, and I decided to help. I didn't know at the time we were related. After hearing my mom was alive, I wanted to find her, so I sent in my DNA to the missing persons registry. That's how I found out we were sisters."

"I'm just happy you're back," her mom said to Alisa. "I've missed you so much." Tears filled her eyes.

"Oh, mom, stop crying," Zora said.

"I can't help it. Thank you, God, for bringing my baby home."

It was still surreal. Her sister was finally back. Sure, they still needed to do a DNA test to confirm their relationship, but Zora already guessed what the result would be.

Zora smiled as she watched her mom with Alisa. Her family was complete, and it was such a great feeling.

They had a lot to discuss and catch up on, but now they had the rest of their lives to do it.

"So what do you do, Alisa?" Zora asked her. By now, her mom had made sure Alisa had demolished the sandwiches Silas had made, along with a glass of sparkling apple cider.

"I'm a corporate lawyer, Harvard-trained. Don't worry, I've always walked on the right side of the law."

Zora smiled at her. The apple didn't fall far from the tree. Alisa had followed in her mom's footsteps.

"What about your family?" Zora asked. "Did you have a sibling?"

Her mom stiffened. She'd probably remembered what the inmate's diary had said about Alisa's kidnapper adopting her. Zora hoped it wasn't true.

Alisa stilled. "I had a brother who used to work at Lexinbridge Regional."

"Really? Was he a doctor?"

Alisa fidgeted. "Yes, he was."

Why was she nervous? Maybe it was something about the brother. "What's his name?"

"Thomas Stewart."

Zora didn't know whether to laugh or cry. The same Thomas Stewart she'd worked with? Come to think of it, she hadn't seen him since her return to the hospital.

"I'm so sorry, Zora," Alisa said.

What did that mean? "What?"

"About what Stewart did to you."

Zora looked at her in confusion. "I don't know what you're talking about."

Alisa stayed silent for a moment. Zora could see the struggle on her face.

"What is it?" Zora said. "Tell me."

"Stewart was behind everything. Sending you to jail and killing your friend."

Zora jumped to her feet. No, it couldn't be true. "Wait! Hold on! What? Why?"

Alisa's face lit up with shame. "He ran the organ trafficking business, and you interfered. I only found out after he died."

Zora shook her head. This was just too much. "He's dead? Why is he dead after killing Marcus?" Zora cried out. "Why Marcus?"

"I heard he had a crush on you, and he hated that Marcus liked you."

Zora collapsed on the seat. Marcus lost his life because of a crush on her? Her heart twisted in pain, and she gasped.

Her mom rushed to her side. "Zora, are you okay?"

"I'm fine. I just…"

"I'm so sorry, Zora. About Marcus and about what happened to you," Alisa said.

"Where's that bastard, Stewart?" a voice said from the stairs.

Zora turned to see Christina coming down. "Can you imagine? He's dead!"

"Why?" Christina said as she reached the bottom and headed in their direction. "Who's this?" she said, gesturing at Alisa. Then she did a double take and stared at her. "She looks just like your mom! Is she…?"

Zora nodded. Even Christina had noticed the resemblance.

Christina's mouth hung open. Then she remembered and closed it. "Hello," she said to Alisa.

"Hello," Alisa replied with a tentative smile.

"That's my best friend," Zora said. "So, back to the subject. Why is Stewart dead?"

"Marcus's uncle killed him," Alisa replied.

Zora looked at her mom. "Marcus had an uncle?"

Her mom nodded. "Yes, he's the head of one of the cartels."

Unbelievable. There was so much she hadn't known. But how was Stewart able to run such an organized organ trafficking business? Unless…

"Who is Stewart's father?" And therefore Alisa's

adopted father, since Stewart was her brother. *Hold on. The man who'd kidnapped Alisa?* Zora glanced at her mom. The same light bulb must have gone off in her mind, because her face tightened.

"Anatoly Petrykin," Alisa said softly.

"The elusive Russian crime boss," Silas stated. "Who would have thought?"

"I'm going to kill him," Alisa's mom said, her face twisted with rage. "First, he kidnaps my daughter, and then his crazy son kills Marcus, who was like a son to me! What did I ever do to him?"

"Adrianna, please calm down," Silas implored.

"How can I? This is just madness! I can't forgive him." She turned to Alisa. "Did he mistreat you?"

Alisa shook her head. "He treated me well," she replied.

"Still, he stole you from me! I just can't let it go," her mom insisted.

"Mom," Zora said. "Think about Alisa."

Her mom turned to Alisa. "I'm sorry, but this is just too much."

"I understand," Alisa said.

Too many revelations tonight, and it would take a few days before everything got sorted. But the most important thing was the miracle had happened. Her sister had come back. Still, after all the years of searching, it was best to start off on the right foot.

"We still need to do a DNA test," Zora said.

Alisa smiled. "I wouldn't expect otherwise, given my profession."

Zora smiled in return. She was glad to have Alisa back. But was she here to stay? Her mom would go mad if she had to share her sister with a crime boss.

"Are you staying?"

The room fell silent at Zora's question.

"If you would have me," Alisa said.

"Of course, honey," her mom said. "We're your family."

"What about the crime boss?" Zora refused to acknowledge that kidnapper as Alisa's father.

"We're never going to see each other again," Alisa said.

Zora felt Alisa's sorrow at her words. It must hurt to cut herself off from someone she'd obviously cared about. The best Zora could do was not speak badly of him, but she could not concede more than that.

"Good," her mom said.

"Oh, one more thing?" Alisa said.

"What is it, honey?" her mom asked.

"Can my dog stay too? I wasn't sure if anyone was allergic to dogs, so I left him outside."

"Why not? Bring the little bugger in," her mom said.

Could Alisa and her mom be more alike? "My mom, or our mom, loves dogs," Zora said to Alisa as they headed to the door. Alisa smiled at Zora's correction. "She just doesn't have time to take care of one. Your dog is about to get spoiled. What's his name?"

"Oh, Sparky is used to being spoiled. He's a little prince."

Zora released the steel door, and Alisa stepped out to retrieve a dog carrier, which held a one-eyed chihuahua.

"He's so cute!" her mother exclaimed as she lifted him out of the bag. Sparky licked her mom's face, and she laughed.

It seemed life in the Smyth house was going to change, after all.

A ringtone buzzed from Zora's pocket. She'd forgotten she still had her mom's phone and pulled it out. It was Dave. Zora needed a little privacy, so she stepped out of the house to take the call. The air was cool, but thankfully, she was wearing a sweater. Still, Zora hoped the conversation wouldn't be long.

"Hello, Dave," Zora said. "I've got good news."

"What is it?"

"My sister just came home."

"What?"

"I know, right? I still can't believe it."

"How do you feel about it?"

"Still in shock. But happy. I don't think it's sunk in yet."

"I'm so happy for you. Are you guys going to do a DNA test?"

"Absolutely. But we already know what the result will be."

"I'd love to drop by and meet her, but you guys need the family time, after enduring so much heartache all these years. Congratulations, Zora."

Zora wiped at the tears that stung her eyes. "Don't make me cry. I'm not ready for it."

"You know it's fine to cry in this kind of situation."

"I know. But I'd rather do it next time. I'm meeting my sister for the first time after many years, and the last thing I'd like to show is a hot mess version of myself." She rubbed at her eyes. "Speaking of which, did you have something to tell me? I'm sure you called me for a reason."

"Yes, it's about the case. Drew Francis, the

patient care assistant, was gone by the time we reached his apartment. A neighbor saw him leaving with a duffel bag. We'd only planned to chat with him, but seeing he'd packed up, we've put out an APB for him. But we don't know yet if we'll be able to catch him. And guess who showed up at the police station?"

"Who?"

"Laura, the Thirst Bar manager. She murdered someone and turned herself in for that. She also claimed she killed Sean Connelly and Eric Sawyer. That she fed them digoxin through their drinks—both men were regular customers at the bar. Oh, and get this: she was the one that dropped the note with the numbers into your hand."

"What's her motive?"

"She says Samantha Pratt, the schoolteacher, was like a daughter to her, and she hated what those men did to the girls. But she's not proficient in computers, and we both know the killer has hacking skills."

"She might be hiding the real killer."

"Hello, Dr. Smyth," an unknown voice said beside her.

Zora started and turned to see a man pointing a gun at her.

It was Drew Francis.

Zora stared into the barrel of a gun.

"Don't think about making any weird moves, or I'll kill you," Drew said. "We're just going to have a nice long chat. Tell them you're going for a walk," he whispered.

Zora turned. Her mom and Alisa were still playing with the dog. Then she felt a gun pressed into the small of her back. "You better hurry, or I might take one of them out just for the fun of it."

Zora knew he could do it too. "Mom, I'm just going to go for a walk, alright?"

"Are you sure?" her mom said. "It's already so late."

Zora gave her mom a warm smile. "It's fine."

"Okay, if you say so," her mom responded, and turned back to the dog.

"See you guys later," she said. "I'll be right back." She hadn't disconnected the call, so Zora was pretty sure Dave had overheard their conversation and was on his way with the cops. She just needed to make sure she stayed alive until they arrived.

Zora turned to Drew. "What next?" For some reason, she remained calm.

"You're going to drop that phone into that shrub over there," he said, pointing to the one he meant. "You didn't think I'd forget, did you?"

Zora's heart sank. She'd hoped he hadn't noticed she was still holding it.

"We're going to take a nice long drive," Drew said as he prodded her to move away from the house. "I hope you said your goodbyes."

"But why me?"

"Why you? You disrupted my mission!"

"What did I do wrong?"

"You had to mess up everything! You told them about my sister's pendant, didn't you?"

So the schoolteacher had been his sister and the owner of the pendant. A tingle of fear went down Zora's back. How had he known?

Drew laughed. "I can see the question in your

face. Of course, I had the police station bugged, just like I bugged your phone. I knew every move your cop friend made. Keep walking, Dr. Smyth," he said as he poked her back with the gun.

Zora stumbled and then righted herself. So Drew was the hacker and the killer behind the digoxin cases. Hopefully, he didn't know Dave was racing to her rescue. She had to keep him occupied, no matter what.

Drew led her toward the trees that stood on the east side of the estate. It seemed he must have somehow found his way onto her parents' property through the grove, which was usually hard to get through. "I disabled the security alarms," he said, answering her unspoken question.

The more they walked through the trees, the more Zora felt her hope draining away. Dave and her family wouldn't know the route they'd taken. She was walking to certain death if she did nothing. In that moment, she wished she'd picked up martial arts instead of boxing, though her current skill level would have been laughable and not enough to fend off Drew.

Zora spied a thick piece of wood lying a few steps away. It could serve as a suitable weapon. All she needed to do was pretend to fall on it, then pick it up as she was rising, and hit him on the head with it. Yes, it could work. She had to take the chance.

She pretended to stumble again and fell on the wood. "Ouch!" she screamed as her hand closed around the wood.

"Dr. Smyth, let go of that weapon." Drew said calmly. "I warned you not to try any funny moves, or I'd kill you. Unfortunately, I keep my promises."

Zora turned to look at him. His face looked serene, but those eyes were like a madman's. He was really going to do it.

Her heart galloped. She would never get to know her sister, and she felt a pang of sorrow at the thought that her mom would gain one child only to lose another.

"Goodbye, Dr. Smyth," Drew leveled the gun at her, his finger reaching to pull the trigger.

Whack! Zora's eyes shut tightly, but then opened when she felt no pain.

She looked up to see Alisa standing behind Drew, who was down unconscious on the ground.

"That was fun," Alisa said as she kicked the gun away.

Zora's shoulders relaxed, the tension draining out of her. She was still alive! "How did you know?"

"I thought it was weird you were going for a walk

at this time of the night, especially since I, your long-lost sister, had just arrived. Then Christina confirmed the same. We figured something was wrong, and I decided it was time to put my extensive martial arts training into good use. I'm just glad I could creep up behind him." She extended a hand out to Zora.

"Thanks for saving me," Zora said as she took Alisa's hand and got to her feet.

"That's what sisters do, right? And from what I gathered from your mom and Christina, you attract a lot of trouble. So I doubt this will be the last time."

"You're quite cheeky, you know."

Alisa grinned. "I aim to please."

Then Zora smiled at her. "What a way to welcome you back to the family."

Alisa smiled back. Then she glanced at where Drew lay. "So, what do we do with him? He's going to be out for at least an hour."

"The cops will be here to take him by then," Zora said. "Let's find something to tie him up."

Fifteen minutes later, Dave and the other cops had arrived, and Zora led them to where they'd tied Drew to a tree. Zora, Silas, and her mom had agreed that it was best to keep Alisa out of what had happened, so she remained upstairs and out of sight.

He was still unconscious where they'd left him. Dave cuffed him and then shook him awake. Another cop picked up the gun Drew had dropped and put it in an evidence bag.

Drew opened his eyes and looked dazed for a moment before he remembered where he was. "Please don't hurt him," he cried out.

"Who's he talking about?" Dave asked Zora.

Zora shrugged. "I have no idea," she said.

"Please leave Andy alone," Drew said. "He's got nothing to do with this!"

"Who's Andy?" Dave asked Drew.

Drew looked at Dave like he'd gone cuckoo. "He is standing over there, of course," he said, gesturing with his head.

Zora looked in the direction Drew was referring to, but there was no one there.

"Andy, stay safe, okay?" Drew continued shouting as they led him to the police car and helped him into it. "I'll be back soon."

Zora watched them take him away.

It was over.

She could have her peace again.

Alisa straightened her dress as she stood before the front door. Her family was waiting for her. She'd gone away for about a week the day after they'd arrested the killer to sort through everything that had happened. Her mom had approved, hoping to have her escape the media's eye till everything had died down. It'd been a time of quiet reflection and contemplation about her future plans. Alisa had also hoped Pete would reach out to her, but he never did.

She'd submitted her DNA for testing, and Zora had texted her to let her know the result was positive, as expected. It'd made everything seem more real.

Once the media clamor had died down, Alisa had

called Zora to let her know she was coming home. Now she was finally here, and it was time.

She let out an exhale. *You'll do fine*, she told herself.

The metal door opened, and Zora stood in the doorway. "You made it," she said with a smile.

Alisa's shoulders relaxed. It was going to be alright. "Yes." Then she chuckled nervously. "It feels strange."

Zora smiled and pulled her into a hug. "You'll do great. Besides, you've met most of us already."

Alisa was still getting used to the fact that she had a big sister now, but she liked the feeling. Of course, there would be times when they disagreed, but she was looking forward to those as well, no matter how exasperating they would turn out to be.

"Come on, let's go in," Zora said. "Everyone is waiting."

Zora led Alisa through the foyer and into the house, still amazed that this was her home where she'd been born and had spent the first few years of her life. She hadn't gotten her memories back and maybe never would, but that was fine. Her family's memories for her were more than enough.

"Surprise!"

Alisa jumped. *Mom, you scared me,* she thought.

It still felt strange calling Mrs. Smyth 'Mom' when Alisa hadn't had one all these years, but it was growing on her.

Her mom headed her way, holding a bouquet of gardenia flowers, her favorite. Of course, her mom would know. She looked so different from the last time Alisa had seen her and was much more relaxed. It still amazed Alisa how much they looked alike.

Alisa had convinced her mom not to press charges against Anatoly Petrykin. As much as Alisa had cut herself from him, he'd loved her in his own way—even more than for his own son—and she couldn't forget that.

"I've never seen Mom this happy," Zora whispered. "She even let her hair down!"

Her mom wrapped Alisa in a hug. "Welcome home," she said, unshed tears glistening in her eyes, her familiar fragrance wrapping around Alisa and warming her.

Yes, she was finally home. And in that moment, a memory of her mom tickling her as a little girl flashed before her eyes.

Alisa gasped.

"Is everything okay?" her mom asked, her eyes searching Alisa's with concern.

Alisa smiled at her. "It's nothing, really. I just had a memory of you."

Her mom's face lit up. "That's good news!" Then she whispered. "Don't worry, I won't tell the others."

"I can hear you, Mom," Zora said.

"You don't count," her mom countered.

Alisa grinned. Only her mom would understand her need to process it on her own first.

"Enough bonding time," Zora said. "Mom, I still need to introduce her to everyone else."

"Alright, alright, she's all yours."

"Thank you."

Zora led Alisa to where the others were waiting around the formal living room. "Alisa, meet Silas, my mom's partner at her firm, and her boyfriend."

Her mom's face turned red. "Did you have to say that?"

Zora shrugged. "It's better she's in-the-know now. Can you imagine how awkward it would be if she caught you guys kissing?"

"Zora!" her mom said.

Silas only chuckled. "Nice to meet you again, Alisa."

Alisa smiled back at him. "Same here."

"Let's move on," Zora said. "And here's

Christina, my BFF, roommate, adopted sister, and all things extraordinaire."

"Hello again," Christina said, and pulled her into a hug. "Now I have another sister."

Alisa liked the sound of that.

Zora then gestured to a tall, handsome bloke standing in the corner. "And that is Brian, my male BFF, and Christina's on-and-off boyfriend."

"You guys are going out?" her mom said as she glanced from Christina to Brian. "How come I'm just hearing about it?"

"Mom, you don't have to know *everything*," Zora said.

"I'm hurt that my adopted daughter didn't tell me," her mom said.

Christina rushed to where Alisa's mom stood and gave her a big hug. "Sorry, Aunt Adrianna."

Her mom chuckled. "Just kidding."

"Lastly, we have Dave." Zora looked around. "Where's Dave?"

"Coming," a voice said from the direction of the kitchen's doorway. He came carrying a tray filled with glasses of sparkling apple cider.

"And this is Dave, my boyfriend," Zora said.

There was a lot of oohing and aahing by everyone.

"Thank goodness you've owned it at last," Christina said. Zora tickled her in response. "Oh, stop it!" Christina cried.

But Alisa stood frozen and stared at Dave.

She knew who he was.

And his name was not Dave.

———

Thank you so much for reading!

Want to know what happens next to Dr. Zora Smyth? You can grab LETHAL ADHESION at https://dobicross.com

If you've loved reading LETHAL RECONCILIATION, Dobi would be grateful if you could spend a few minutes to leave a review (as short as you like) on the book's page on your favorite retailer. Your review would help bring it to the attention of other readers. Thank you very much.

Check out all Dobi Cross books at https://dobicross.com

ACKNOWLEDGMENTS

Writing a book is harder and more rewarding than I could have ever imagined. And it would not have been possible without the support, love, and encouragement from my number one cheerleader, my dearest mom. My life would never have been this awesome and wonderful without you.

Of course, I have to thank my precious little DC for his smiles and antics. You brighten my day and give me the strength to keep pushing through.

Thank you to my sisters for encouraging me on this wonderful journey. And a special thanks to my baby brother (who is so not a baby anymore) for being super supportive and checking in on my progress. You guys are the best.

Thank you to my wonderful author friends. You know who you are. Your selflessness and willingness to share what you know has made my writing journey smoother and an exciting one. And a special thanks to Lisa and Deanna whose support have made a difference.

Most of all, I want to thank God who gave me life, surrounded me with the most wonderful people, and loved me all the way. You make my life complete.

And finally, a special thanks to all my readers whose love of my stories spur me on to write more. Thank you!

ABOUT THE AUTHOR

As a former physician and business executive in another life—with a childhood filled with reading multi-genre novels (including Shakespeare in the original version)—Dobi Cross loves to write thrilling stories with heart.

She enjoys dreaming up everyday characters who rise above unfavorable circumstances to overcome incredible odds. When not writing, Dobi can be found binging K-dramas and ice cream with her little sidekick by her side.

Lethal Reconciliation is the fourth book in the Dr. Zora Smyth Medical Thriller Series. Sign up at https://dobicross.com to be notified when the next Dobi Cross book comes out!

Thanks for reading LETHAL RECONCILIATION!

https://dobicross.com
hello@dobicross.com
facebook.com/dobicrossauthor
bookbub.com/profile/dobi-cross
instagram.com/dobicross